Glow in the Dark

For Doreen Anderson Wood,

All the best,

Lisa Teasley

Glow in the Dark

Lisa Teasley

 Cune

Glow in the Dark
Cune Press, Seattle, 2002

First Edition
3 5 7 9 10 8 6 4 2

"What the Fertility Goddess Brought" appeared in *Rampike*. "Holiday Confessional" appeared in *Washington Square*, "Why I Could Never Be Boogie" appeared in *Great River Review*. "The Breaking of Miss and Mrs. Gaines" appeared in *Event*, and "White Picket Fence" appeared in *Amelia*. "Nepenthe" appeared in *Herstory*. "Baker" appears in the anthology *Step Into a World: A Global Anthology of the New Black Literature*.

Individuals:
Copies of *Glow in the Dark* are available for purchase at your local independent bookstore. Also available online or toll free: www.cunepress.com; (800) 445-8032.
Bookstores:
Find the Cune Press Catalogue at www.cunepress.com.

Cune Press
PO Box 31024
Seattle, WA 98103
www.cunepress.com

We wish to thank the Allied Arts Foundation for its support.

For John

Thank You

Montserrat Fontes and Jascha Kessler. Joel Rose, Karen Rinaldi, Kevin Powell, and Meri Nana-Ama Danquah. Matthew Bialer, Leslie Gardner, Dave Dunton and Ira Silverberg. Pearl Cleage, Jabari Asim, Wanda Coleman, and Danny Simmons. John Kaplan, Joseph Gallo, Robert Lyons and Ron Dobson. Terri Patchen, Hooman Majd, Bill Brown, Daniel Baxter, Ron Athey, Traci Lind, David Trinidad, Austin Young, Eric Junker, Kateri Butler, Christian Puffer, Frederic Cassidy, Kathleen Wiegner, Aldo Sampieri, Roger Neal, Scott C. Davis, and Yoona Lee. Laura, Erica, Violet and Larkin Teasley, Casey and Willy Vlautin. Imogen Teasley-Vlautin.

Contents

New York

Baker

The last person ever to see Marty naked was his little sister, Baker, back in Amarillo, Texas when they were 12 and 5, respectively. Not long after, Baker was diagnosed as autistic. Marty always thought his nakedness had caused his sister's disability.

Marty moved to New York when he was 17. For nine years he had numerous jobs involving grease and oil, until he met Carol who hired him at the paper in Jersey City, where he lived. Carol was soon fired but it didn't matter since she failed upwards. She had already been fired from seven jobs, each one paying more than the last, so she sported no pallor of defeat. Carol was beautiful—not heartbreakingly beautiful, but beautiful and heartbreaking. Only 33, she'd been divorced three times. The ex-husbands hung on, left messages on the machine. Marty knew little about them because he didn't want to. She told Marty her lovers had always worn jockeys, but her mates wore boxers. Marty looked particularly tall, skinny, pale, and gangly in the boxers she chose for him. Although it had been a year and a half with Carol, he was always half-dressed with the lights off when they had sex, and he always took showers with the door locked. So she'd never seen him naked. This she said she'd conquer after he agreed to go to AA.

As well as drinking there was coffee to kick, then sugar, then Jesus. Soon Marty found the god of health. Couple mornings a week when he had spent the night at Carol's in Williamsburg, he'd leave the car in front of her building, and take the L train one stop into the city for yoga on 1st and 15th. There was a woman, Leila, whom he somehow didn't consider a revisiting of his past big black girl fetish. This was different, and serious. He could never predict which class she would attend, but when he was lucky, he'd walk in, see her name on the sign-in sheet, and anticipate the thrill of watching her limbs move, her muscles skate, her dark skin shine. Her body had one flaw which didn't challenge aesthetic but rather function. When she scooped her stomach on the floor, pressing the palms of her long hands, attempting to bring herself up into the position called Cobra, she winced, hardly making it halfway. He heard her apologize many times to the teacher for the structure of her spine. He wanted badly to hear her whisper the same into his ear while fucking her from behind. But he knew this would take time.

Marty's sponsor gave him a tape denouncing self-will, self-love, and sex. Mornings after Carol rode him, he would pop the cassette in her deck while she got ready for work. But this time Carol came out of the bathroom and screamed. When he showed no reaction, she started yelling about how nice it was when they first met, listening to tapes of the ocean, or some of the "fast shit" that he was into when she still worked at the paper. Watching her, Marty felt nothing. He wondered how he'd ever fell for her, since he had never really liked the taste of her. She ran for the iron which wasn't plugged in, scrambled for him where he sat on the bed, then punched him with it in the ear. The pain rang as he closed his palm over his ear. He looked up at her in disbelief, and then she hit him again, this time in the jaw, which was where she said she'd meant to put the first one.

He could knock her back with it, or he could lie there enjoying the pain and the look of girlish regret on her face. He'd seen it before when she'd hit him, but these scattered incidents of her explosive anger were few and far between. The pain felt right, he thought, burying the back of his head into the pillow as Carol said she was sorry, and put her hands gently on Marty's hips. Forgive me, she said. And he knew he was forgiven for one more night of sex that meant nothing to him, for one more night of sex without love or marriage. How was it, he wondered, had these ex-husbands fallen for her anyway?

The drive through the Holland Tunnel, the stop and start and the echoing howls of horns made him aware for the first time that they were all under water. It felt soothing to him. He could live out the fantasy of drowning, if he really concentrated, and it would squeeze it out, those thoughts of little girls, and the whackings, as he called them, from his old mother.

What happened to your face? everybody in the building

kept asking as he made his rounds with the mail. And everybody, except Benjamin, got the sly smile from Marty which hurt and reminded him. With Benjamin he went out to the truck for a dog and a Snapple. Both tasted nasty and cancelled out all of last week's offerings to the god of health.

Marty my man, have you fallen off? Benjamin finally asked from the curve where they sat looking across the street to the soot-colored building. Ah nah, man, 246 days, I'll make it to my first birthday, Marty said, smiling to face Benjamin, so it hurt again. It was Carol, and I didn't lay a hand on her. Benjamin shook his head, laughed, then said, Don't take this the wrong way, but everybody knows, me especially, that Carol is fucked up. Marty rolled that over for a while, then said, No, it's me. Really. Well, Benjamin said, This is the best time of year to count your friends and leave the rest of them where they belong, in the dirt. Know what I mean, man? When the leaves are changing color, and falling down on the ground. The beauty of it man, always tells the truth. Yeah, Marty answered. I used to travel 'round this time most every year. Drive from Texas to wherever when the colors were doing their thing. And I used to leave half my heart home, but then came a time when I took the whole thing with me. So I know what you mean. Maybe you do, man, Benjamin said. And then again, maybe you don't, because you have this problem, see, with listening. Benjamin got up and hit him firmly on the back of the head, and called back, See you in there.

Later when Marty drove by the preschool, and his head started pounding, pushing, trying to squeeze out any too-old memories of his little sister Baker, he ran a red light then screeched all the way to the first payphone to call his sponsor.

Thomas, a market analyst, had given him his cell number, and whenever Thomas gave him a short quick response of when he could call him back, Marty knew that when Thomas did call, Marty would have to wait out five minutes of a testy edge until Thomas settled in with some humanity. Fuck it, Marty said aloud when he hung up, and he made it to the next meeting.

While he was there not listening to the woman going on about her sickness, he was thinking he would go to a yoga class for every meeting. That would up his chances for seeing Leila.

It was the fourth time when Leila gave him five minutes after class, and he gave her the depth of his white boy humility, which had always worked. He asked if he could drive her home since she lived in Brooklyn. Even though he didn't have his car there, he knew she would turn him down but maybe take him up on it the next time. So he figured out her schedule. He found out she was a pastry-maker for a French restaurant in the city, and he feigned surprise, lied and said his mother did the same thing in San Francisco. It occurred to him he should explain his slight Texas twang, so he told her about Amarillo but made up the rest about moving to California with his mother, and he left out his sister all together. There was some truth to it, he thought. The instructor said goodbye, and a couple of people pushed in to get their things, as Leila pulled her skirt up over her purple bike shorts, now covering the shape of her gorgeous thighs. She slipped her backpack on quickly. This lie wasn't such a stretch, Marty thought. After all, his mother worked in a diner and pies were among the things she served, and his mother had a sister who left for California soon after their parents were murdered when his mother and aunt were still in their teens.

From the door of the building, Marty decided to go the opposite way of Leila, so he could wait until she made it three quarters of a block, then follow her. When she disappeared down the steps into the subway, he walked around in search of a lingerie shop to buy her a bra and panties, some deep strain of red, like burgundy or maroon, that would set off the tone of her skin. Then he could give it to her at the proper moment.

Carol had been leaving desperate messages on his machine for the past week, since he'd only been by her place once or twice in the last month. The time before last was violent again. He swore to her later he didn't mind, because he knew it saved him from having to have sex with her again, and again.

Sponsor Thomas invited Marty to meet him at one of his Wall Street bars thick with slick hair and cigar smoke. How can you drink Coke in one of these places? Marty asked him as he always did. Because I have to, Thomas said, it's my job. And that's what you have to learn, Marty, how to handle yourself in all the tough situations, like bars, and women, and lonely winter nights. This winter hasn't been shit yet, has it? Marty asked trying to be light. No it hasn't, Thomas said, dragging on his cigarette. So tell me, you moving up yet in that shit-hole of a paper? Marty laughed. And then he looked past him, and made a tunnel through all of the dark suits, and loud voices that sounded like one long grumble until Marty squeezed it into a rumble, fast, like getting into a car and racing it down the road, dragging it past the drunk fucks who'd just challenged him to a crash.

What do you see in me? Marty asked Thomas. Thomas laughed, and then squinted his eyes, and brought his face closer to Marty's, and with a slim curl in his lip, whispered, Is there something you're trying to tell me, son? Then he winked, hit the table, beating it with both hands as if it were a drum, and said, Fuck man, you're going to make it.

The eighth time Marty had a treasured encounter with Leila was when she finally said she would take that ride home. They had to walk five blocks to his car, and he noticed she often left off the last words of her sentences, as if he was supposed to know what would come next. He noticed too that there was something similar to Carol about her, not their skin or texture of their hair, of course, but something in the space between all of the features of their face. He was sorry about this and tried to see something else. He concentrated then on the expression she had with the instructor when he would adjust her, this kind of merciful expression he wanted to lick off.

As they drove, he was relieved to see that she lived in Park Slope, very mixed, and not some black ghetto he couldn't be caught dead in in Texas. And he pushed that out of his mind as well. He was determined not to fuck with his own mind and his own past with her, because he deserved a little better this time.

It wouldn't be right to come in, he thought, as he pulled up in front of her building, and she gave him the sweetest smile of gratitude. Then something else washed across her face just before she opened the door, and he wanted to slap it off her. That thought scared him, as she said, Thank you, and got out, and she shoved the door closed quite hard, and since his car had human qualities to him, he took offense for a moment, then thought to himself, Well she could never know what a car could mean, she's probably never owned one in her life.

He saw Carol that night and she'd pulled out all the stops, candlelight, very sheer nylons, and she even put on his favorite gloves, and sat dangling her shoe from the tip of her toes, the way he used to love. Instead of grabbing her as he thought he would a moment ago, he got up, proud of himself, feeling like Thomas, whom he realized he hated and had always hated, but felt proud to be like as he walked out the door. Yes, he did know how to handle difficult situations.

At the truck with Benjamin the next day in front of work, Marty said it was finally over with Carol. Thank God, man, Benjamin said gulping down his Sprite, pulling his pea coat tight around his neck. I was beginning to think you were truly thick, but you did it man. Marty smiled, leaned back, and stretched his arms behind him. Benjamin started talking about Hawaii again, where his stepfather had an old coffee ranch, and what it was like the last time he was there and how he wished he was there right then. And then he started talking about his best friend from college, with whom he'd had some rivalry that started with some chick but was really about something deeper like the dynamics of his family. Marty tuned out, and headed to the preschool in his mind. When he realized Benjamin had gotten up, he looked up at him and saw that Benjamin was looking at him with disgust. See you in there, man, Benjamin said, as if to hide the look. But Marty saw it. He never missed those looks. He'd seen them way too often in most everybody he knew.

Leila had been to lunch with him once, then for a late coffee one Thursday night. It wasn't until after a movie, the week of his first birthday, that he decided to give her the underwear. It was daring, seeing as how he had never even kissed her, and he felt a punch in the gut as he handed her the package, all wrapped in butcher paper with a curly yellow ribbon.

I'll open this when I get home, if you don't mind, she said to him. She was searching his eyes, the way he hates in a woman. Why do they always do that, exactly when you don't want them to? Marty looked at the ground, and then they got in his car and he drove her home playing the "fast shit" Carol would have preferred to his self-help tapes.

He didn't see Leila until two weeks later when he picked her up one morning to go to yoga. She came down the steps with a little girl, and the sight of her knocked him flat. As Leila opened the door, Marty thought he was having a breathing attack. Leila ignored it, or else didn't see it, and she introduced the little girl. He didn't get her name, but he did hear that she was her daughter. When he was catching his breath, looking out of his window, pretending to watch for oncoming traffic before he pulled out, Leila said they needed to drop her daughter off at dance class, and her cousin would be picking her up.

Marty heard nothing else Leila said that whole excruciating drive to the dance class, which couldn't have been more than five minutes but took him through his entire lifetime in his head. He kept trying not to look at her, there in the backseat, her hands in her lap. Looking out of the window, then at him in the rearview mirror, she was already like an adult with that subtle look of disgust on her lips.

He watched Leila take her to the door, and then come out again. She looked as if she were trying to catch her breath too, and before she got in, it seemed for a moment as if she were changing her mind.

I should have told you about her, I suppose. No, no, Marty said, and then he wondered where that came from, out of him. I mean, I had plenty of opportunities, and I mussed them all. He looked at her before they got on the bridge, and then he thought he should try and be nice. As they began to climb it, he put his hand over hers, but more to steady his own mind. You don't have a problem with children, do you? she asked hesitantly, and her eyes were big, and he hated that, and then hated her for making him think he could push her out of the car and head for the first bar. Just a few weeks after his birthday, like that. No, no, Marty said. How old is she, anyway? Four and a half, she said. A big four and a half. I wouldn't know, Marty said, too quickly. The traffic started to bunch up and he felt smothered being up so high. She doesn't look much like you. Thanks, she said. Then she laughed. Her father is Pakistani. Really? Marty asked, moving the gear into park, as traffic had come to full stop for minutes on end. They don't like black people much, Indians, do they? She seemed taken aback at this, and then she laughed again. Well, who does like black people much? Sorry, Marty said, looking at her. Forget it. You don't want to hear the history with her father, which is very much over for me. Not for her. He's actually a good man, and we were in love for some time. It just didn't work is all. Sorry, Marty repeated, and then moved back into gear to crawl another few feet. Shyly she looked at him, You think we'll make it to class? Probably not, he said, relaxing finally. Well, she said. She laid her head back on the seat. She sighed. She looked out of the window. Well, she said again. I must tell you, I fell asleep in the underwear you gave me. She turned to look at him, and so he returned it. You can't guess what I dreamed, she said. Maybe I can, Marty said, getting mesmerized by her eyes, then turning to drive a few more feet. I'll tell you anyway, her smile getting bigger, her eyes more coy. I dreamed you fucked me all night. Well, Marty said. Well, well. Leila gasped a little before she giggled, and it touched him. That being the case, Marty said, if I've already had you, I may as well have you. And they drove through the traffic on the bridge and through the streets, and through the Holland Tunnel to his place in Jersey City.

I have a new woman now, Marty said to Thomas after a meeting. Thomas shook his head, as he lit a cigarette. Marty's breath was thick in front of him, as thick as the smoke Thomas blew to the side before he responded, What did I tell you about women? I know what you told me, Marty said, But I wasn't born this morning. No, Thomas said, you were born a little over a year ago when you took your last drink. Maybe so, Marty said, Nevertheless, this isn't about sex. This is something entirely different. I'm feeling as new and as pure as I did before I ever had a filthy thought in my head. Is that so, Thomas said, laughing. Well, my friend, if that is truly the case, you're going against everything in the program. You aren't tough enough to lick this thing over night. Get it into your head, my man. You are an alcoholic. And after only little more than a year of sobriety, you are nowhere near knowing one from two, much less twelve. Be careful, Thomas said, as he turned to walk off. Then he stopped in his tracks, looked back at Marty, and called, And consider this woman, my friend, she deserves someone who still has his head! Marty flipped him off, and Thomas brought up his hands, like, What else can I say? then kept walking.

It was early summer by the time Leila could trust Marty longer than 20 minutes alone with her girl. He was in her room, and she was showing him her latest action figure, which went with the one he just gave her. Leila would only be an hour getting her hair "touched up" at the salon. She had someone fast, she said, yet she said this more to bolster her own confidence, it seemed to him, than to reassure him of the shortness of any babysitting duties. The girl had him laughing over the toughness with which she fought his doll with hers. The games in her head seemed complicated to him, and it brought him back to his little sister Baker, but instead of squeezing it out, he tried to remember how it was when it was good and natural between them. He relaxed with it, laughed, and enjoyed himself, and so it caught him by surprise when she said she had to go to the bathroom, and he found himself following her. I don't need help, she said, as she started to close the door. But when he put his hand there to stop her from closing it, startled, she looked up at him.

He couldn't hear whatever he said to her so that she would just relax and go ahead and pull her pants down and "go potty," that part he did hear himself say, but he couldn't see himself, or he couldn't imagine himself doing what he was doing, as he was taking off all of his clothes to be completely naked while the girl wasn't looking but busying herself with the toilet paper. She had pulled off too much of the toilet paper, and when she saw that he was nearly naked, she asked too loudly what he was doing, so he moved over to her to cover her mouth. Oh God, he thought, because his mind was trying to catch up to him, something didn't feel right, as everything was clearing up and he began to see a bit of himself, and the terror was starting but he had to rush on through. The girl was struggling with all she had in her, and so when he heard the door open, a part of him was set free and the other part panicked, trying to push his body against the bathroom door, trying to keep it closed, while trying to hold onto the girl's mouth, and her body, while he heard Leila wailing and kicking at the door, and everything all slippery with his sweat. There were stomps on the floor and then Leila was back again. She got the door open, and there she stood with a gun, pointed at his nose, while she yanked the child from him, threw her out of the room and closed the door behind her. *Yes,* Marty heard himself say, as she cocked it.

Holiday Confessional

The girl is not dead. She is coughing blood as Pup and Zasu bolt from the lot where she lies. Slowing up, they turn the corner, begin humming in harmonic thump, keeping steady pace.

In that hat ribboned with the print of grasshoppers, is Olga. She's in her usual spot, and just as drunk. She nods, they nod. A freak July flip of wind lifts her hat, and it jumps the curb. Olga bends the wrong way as they pass, and she won't remember seeing them. They speed up two beats down Grand Avenue, reach Zasu's door.

Pup pats his heart.

"You comin' in?" Zasu asks, merengue pumping down the hall.

"No way."

"Just don't do anything stupid, Pup man."

"Catch you tomorrow."

Pup waits for the click of the lock, then he runs.

On the payphone seven blocks from Zasu's, Pup dials 911, tells them the cross streets, Driggs and Fillmore. He hangs up, heads for the L. Hurting his brain is the hot pink of her gums, the knob of her throat going up and down, her face not matching what he'd heard blast the air from a few yards away, *"You'll have to kill me first!"*

To catch the train he vaults the stile, jumps four steps a time, shoves his arm in to the elbow, pries open the doors. The old woman, probably Polish, swallows heavily and touches her lizard neck. She holds her bag closer, stares up at the ads. She glares once again at him; he sits too narrowly in her vision. He looks down at his hands folded in his lap, and then he too is afraid of himself.

For the first time in months, Pup thinks of heading to the Port Authority for the Jersey bus to see Millie. She'll slick her impeccably straightened hair in place as he follows her into the kitchen. She'll feed him something with lentils, unless she's obsessing on another protein. She'll ask few questions because she hasn't wanted to know for years. She'll bitch about not being promoted beyond director of personnel. She'll show him the news in her garden, praise the quality of her dirt. She'll protest little when he says he can't stay. Before he leaves, he'll grab from her stash of almond M&Ms, and he'll call her Mama to hurt her, drum up regret.

Pup and his twin brother Pace, twelve years old then, living with their father in LA, spending most holidays with their mother Millie in New York, and this particular summer, Millie nine months pregnant with a half sister the father eventually took away. The night before, Millie crying over his and Pace's father. How much she still loved him, she said. She mentioned nothing about wanting Pup and Pace back. Then the next day Pup coming in on Millie, *their mother,* and Pace. She hungrily caressing the half-circle of his cheek to his sharp jaw to the cushion of his lips. His lips were on her nipple, and she was squeezing it. Later she gave Pup a separate talking to. What you saw, she said, was nothing. Pace was just curious about the taste of milk. But what I'd like from now on is for you both to stop calling me Mama. That's what I'd like, she repeated, before they left.

Looking up at a zit cream ad, Pup feels the train rumble and squeal to a halt. He doesn't hear why they'll move again in a minute, because he's hearing the girl again, seeing the girl lying there. Zasu yanking him by the shirt, and yelling in hot whispers to him, the girl holding her throat, turning her head from side to side and it's hypnotizing him, her one thigh jerking up and down with the shakes. The panties are in a delicate twist on her ankle, like a bracelet.

Pup hard now, a nasty taste takes his tongue, and he won't throw up. The train snaps him into shame, and he jolts up, unnecessarily crowding the door, waiting to get out. His eyes flit from one First Avenue sign to the next. Finally the doors slide open and he flings himself free. He flies three steps a time into city-lit dark and he imagines trying to get through another night. Loneliness knits his gut into knots, and he yearns for day and the shape and strength of his father's arm pointing out the sun dog on the horizon. He hears his father's voice, telling him to look at the metal, wire, crack vials, and broken glass in conscious argument with the sky. Lately he's found himself on the same corner around four in the afternoon to watch the pigeons circle the roof, the light hitting their wings golden so that they look like individual churches.

Down First, passing through pockets of dealers and the ruthless howls of sirens, Pup kicks the shreds of clothes lying on the sidewalk, squints his eyes until lights collapse into clusters. He puckers his nose at the pulpy stench of trash, turns the corner at St. Marks, and descends the steps of the Holiday Bar. Two girls sit at the end. They are laughing with the bartender who's drunk. One is black with platinum blonde dreadlocks, the other white, neither of them really fine. Then again, neither is he. Pup never shined like Pace. Pup was named for his father, Paul; Pace, for their grandfather. Both Paces are dead now.

After Pup's second beer he moves to the empty seat next to the white girl. The air doesn't change. She's too thin, pale with long dust-colored hair, her breasts lost in an oversized short-sleeved polka dot shirt. Her arms glow as she scribbles from one long list on a napkin to another.

"What are you writing?" Pup asks, trying to control the nervous habit of opening his eyes wide then blinking rapid fire.

"An ex-boyfriend's mother's recipe for spinach enchiladas," she answers, not looking up.

The blonde dread takes a sip. He can't see her body with the white one in the way. She moves her hair back, there is a mole moments under her left cheekbone, her eyes widely spaced apart. She takes him in softly, then lets him go.

"So how do you make spinach enchiladas?" Pup asks, staring at the white one's knuckles as they vibrate.

"Just a second, I'm recopying it. Can barely read my

own writing."

A guy pushes in between Pup and the white girl. He asks the bartender for a beer, but the bartender ignores him and moves to the other side of the counter. Knocking into Pup the guy leaves to follow the bartender before Pup can flirt with his anger. The blonde dread watches Pup ready to spring, then she puts her elbow on the counter, rests her chin in her hand, as if it were him, and it calms him down.

"So your ex-boyfriend's mother . . . " Pup begins again with the white one.

"Yeah, I called her a few minutes ago, she owns two restaurants in LA, and since we're having a party tomorrow . . . "

"I grew up in LA," Pup cuts her off, hurrying a bit more excitedly than he'd meant. "Long Beach. My father still lives there. He's an artist."

"Really," she says lazily, looking up at him finally. Her eyes are corraded silver. "I've probably been to Long Beach once."

She turns to the blonde dread, moves the lock back that has slipped into her drink, then lovingly touches her earlobe. It is fat, with no rings, no holes, and he would like to suck it.

"Get me another one, will you, when he comes this way," the white one says, leaning into the counter to stick the napkins in her back pocket. She gets up and he won't turn to see her ass.

"My name's Paul," he says, offering his hand to the dread. Her highly arched, comic strip-like eyebrows suddenly meet, perched for flight.

"Paula," she says, and laughs. She shakes him once firmly, her hand wet from the glass.

"Nice to meet you," he says.

The dread flashes her teeth, he sees her dark gums, and then he sees the hot pink gums. Pup squeezes his eyes shut, his head again tracking that voice, *You'll have to kill me first!"*

"Something wrong?" the dread asks him. Pup opens his eyes.

The white one is back, the sound as she slips onto the chair reminds him of butterflies.

"Something wrong there, handsome?" the white one says. Pup's nostrils involuntarily flare because everything the white one says comes off like she doesn't mean it.

"His name's Paul," the dread says.

"How sweet. Paul and Paula. Let me see your profile Paul," the white one says, grabbing Pup's chin with her cold hand. She is smiling with those silver eyes that now flicker. "This profile should be on a coin, don't you think? Or at least on a stamp."

"Buy me a beer and I'll forget you touched me without asking," Pup says.

"Ooooo. That's fair," she says, waving her hand at the bartender. "My name is Virgie, by the way, and it's a pleasure."

The blonde dread crinkles her nose then lets it smooth with her mouth into welcome. Pup looks at her then back at the white girl who is softening as she tilts her head to the side. The polka dots ricochet from her shirt as she moves toward him to steady herself on her seat. She suddenly becomes pretty in a way that says, Trust me.

"I had my first flying dream in a long time," Pup says, taking a swig of the beer.

"I hate my flying dreams," the white one says, "they usually end with me in some auditorium giving class instruction.

I make it just over the audience then someone pulls me down."

"No one ever sees me," Pup says. "I take off from a different bedroom window each night. It's hard at first to make the height. I scrape trees then I make it over buildings, struggling the whole time. It's never weightless, the flight. And when I land I'm cut up and bruised, and I've got this yellow cornmealy shit in my mouth that I end up digging with my hands because it's not enough to spit it out."

"You should keep your mouth shut when you fly," the white one says.

"Like I said, I haven't flown in a long time," Pup says, putting both hands on the counter. The color of dirt, his hands. He thinks of Millie in her garden, praising the smell. I have good dirt, Millie says, Look at it, so dark. The darker the soil the richer, she says.

The girls are talking to each other, the beer grabbing at his head. The song on the jukebox stutters, somebody kicks it back in place.

Look at me Pace, Pup whispers to himself. He wonders what Pace could have said before they beat him to death. He remembers that night how he felt it. One of the few times he'd slept the last few years in a comfortable bed. He woke up to the chorus of blood rushing the sockets of his eyes. His head buried in the pillow, tears sizzling his ear.

"Want another one John Paul?" the white one says.

"Who said my name was *John* Paul?"

"No one. I'm thinking of the Pope, I'm thinking of my father. Bartender, hit us again!" the white one says, slapping the counter. She raises a brow at Pup, then smiles. She leans back so that her hair is dusting the waist of her jeans. She leaves a view to the dread's body, unforgivably lush, and suddenly together they look like a billboard. The dread smiles too, looks at Pup, then back at her friend.

Against his blue Hawaiian shirt, and brass white hair, the bartender's liver shows on his face. His forehead and brow in a permanent claw of concern, he pours the dread more water, more whiskey, puts down two more beers. Pup looks up at the deer head with candycane, buttons, Mardi Gras beads hanging from its antlers. He can't hear what the white one tells the bartender. The bartender puts up his arms as if she might shoot, then walks away.

"Now, tell us something good, John Paul," the white one says, bumping the barlight with her face.

"Okay. My mother was a Black Panther," he answers.

"Oh really," the white one says, her thin bottom lip curling as if she had rolled her eyes. "Lot of children of Panther mothers running around these days."

The blonde dread laughs, and tenderly with one finger wipes the corner of her mouth.

"Don't be like that," Pup says, not knowing why he lied. He stares at the shape of her skull.

"Okay, tell us about your mother."

"Forget about my mother. Forget I mentioned her. Let's talk about my father. You would both *love* my father," Pup says.

"Is that right? Is he as handsome as you?" the white one asks.

Pup directs his attention to the dread.

"If he were here right now, he'd take us above . . . the dirt."

"Well not my father," the white one interrupts, "the Jesus

freak. He nearly killed me."

"Don't knock Jesus. Jesus was cool," Pup says.

"Oh please," the white one interrupts, "do not explicate."

"My partner's named for him, Hay-soos, but since his baby sister pronounced it Zasu, the name stuck."

"Zasu, huh?" the white one grabs his hand, squeezes it. "I love what babies do with a name. I had a baby. Oh you can't imagine what it feels like to be pregnant," the white one exclaims, letting go of his hand to put hers up in the air in the shape of a V. The dread straightens her back and looks at the counter as if waiting for her friend to finish quickly. "It's beautiful, you know. When the baby kicked it felt like waves instead of blows. Like I had this ocean inside me. But then there was him, the Jesus freak."

The guy that had knocked into Pup returns to ask the bartender to spot him a five. The bartender's eyes go navy and slit. Pup watches his brass white hair whiz under the counter as he rabidly growls at the guy to get the fuck out of his bar. The bartender is small and packed tight in a bundle in the guy's face as he appears to consider whether he might hit the guy. Pup gets up to back the bartender. The dread grabs his arm, her nails sinking into his skin.

"You just stay out of other people's shit, Paul, if you know what's good for you. Just leave it alone," the dread says, taking an evil tone.

"Oh really, is that what I should always do?" Pup says, matching it. "And what's your story anyway? You haven't said a fucking thing this entire time."

"Nevermind all that, and don't curse at me. I only said don't start any shit around me, okay?" the dread says, putting her hands up, the nails long and fake and ready to be plucked.

The white one's face is fraught with interest.

"Listen, don't pound on me, tonight." Pup says, his eyes blinking too fast.

"Pound?"

"Don't pound on me," he says, working his spit.

"Simmer down there John Paul," the white one says.

"You say to me, 'Stay out of other people's shit,' and that's exactly what I've done tonight," Pup says, both palms slamming the counter.

"What the hell is he talking about?" the dread says, expanding her chest.

"I didn't do it! I didn't rape her," he says, shaking from the gut, his eyes flooding.

"Jesus Christ . . . " the dread says.

"I *'stayed out of other people's shit,'* and maybe she's dead because of it," his shakes moving up to the shoulders. "I stayed out of it. We hear the girl screaming, we *wait,* then see the mutha'fuckahs running, and when we get there, we see her, torn up, raw and bleeding. And what do we do? Zasu man, what do we do? We walk the fuck *away!"* Pup begins knocking himself with the heels of his palms, first the forehead, the eyes, the cheeks, the chin, then he holds his own throat, bares down until someone tries pulling his hands away.

"Take it outside, come on, calm yourself down," somebody says.

"Hold on a minute," he thinks the white one says. He hears the mumbling and the rumbling, he tries shutting them up, cutting them off.

"That's right, you heard me exactly right!" Pup says,

snapping with his teeth, breathing in hard to keep the snot from running with the tears. He feels the hands again, firm on his biceps, trying to lift him. "Who knows if we'd stayed . . . who knows, man, I mean how many *minutes* it takes. Worrying about our own asses. Around there, mutha' fuckahs hacking up people with machetes for whatever kind of shit . . . "

He hears the girls, then the hands let him go. Someone moves out of the way.

"But it was some dumb-as-fuck and just as guilty piece-of-shit that did the same thing with Pace, just walked away, like I did from that girl, and now Pace is dead," Pup finishes, now only his jaw shaking, his breathing finding a steadier rhythm as he holds onto the counter, then tries squeezing it from his head. Images curdle his brain. He feels his father holding him from behind, not hearing what comes out of the priest's mouth, then he sees Millie throwing a handful of dirt into Pace's grave. Then Millie scooping up more dirt and throwing it all around, some of it hitting Pup in the face. He sees them holding onto Millie as she's trying to knock everybody down, then he registers what is actually in front of him, the open mouth of the dread looking frantic, and the white one leaning into him, about to touch him, an expression of confusion on her face.

"Who, John Paul, is Pace?" she calmly asks.

Pup gets up, kicks his stool over, hears the growling behind and the rumble as he shoves open the aluminum door. As he jumps the three steps in one outside to fresh air, the Christmas lights in the bar remain in his head. Suddenly they turn into fireflies, swoop up, circle, then finally get away.

Wanting Girlfriend with the Pink Hair

Every morning, same thing, waking up to his sister Emerald's nose in his ass because she loves the smell, it's easy for her, he naked and always ending up on stomach, spread eagle, and like a cat Emerald is up first, in his bed, her nose in his ass, perhaps in tribute to their mother who, laughing, used to wake them up this same way, sometimes grabbing his balls, Emerald's buds, and saying, "My precious stones," that's why he changed his name, because of their mother, her obsession with precious stones, naming him Zinc which he changed to Cy, short for Cyrus, but Emerald holding onto Emerald, as Cy'll call her Emery, short for Emery Bored, though she is nothing of either kind.

"What's this Cy? Two pimples on your ass."

"Get off of me," Cy answers, as always, into the pillow.

"Oh, lemme at 'em."

Too late, he's kicked her to the floor, quickly gets up, scratching his head, cupping his balls, heading for the head. Emerald is on her first Mint Julep of the morning, the drink of the week, always a new drink of the week every morning since the opening of the bar, almost a year ago.

"What in the world could that line be for?" Emerald calls from the window overlooking the Public Theater on Lafayette, but Cy doesn't answer since he hasn't seen it yet.

"You can't tell from this crowd," she says, scratching her head, licking the sugar from her lips. "You can never tell anymore from these crowds, can you? Cy? Come over here, and talk to me."

"Too sweet, really," he says, giving the drink back to her. "It's a wonder I let you do any mixing, a wonder anyone ever comes back to the bar."

Cy digs his foot into one of the many scarves on the floor, one of the *hundreds* of pieces of material Emerald finds, swearing she'll sew some outfit together, but mostly buying everything she passes on the street she fancies and can barely afford. Cy sits down to the baby grand, begins the Bach piece he's been working out for the past few weeks, as Emerald grinds the beans, puts his coffee on.

"I thought that puppet thing was starting this week. That couldn't be the line for the puppet thing, could it? Cy?"

His eyes are closed. She opens the window, sticks her head out, her pink hair shining strangely gray in the morning light, her finger in her ear, plugging out his music, digging for wax.

"What?" she asks as if he had said anything to her. "Cy? Come over here a minute, would you?"

Emerald spins around, pulls the end of her T-shirt down to cover her thigh, measures with her fingers the distance of its limits from her knee.

"My legs are too short, really. They are much too short. Why couldn't I have gotten your legs? Cy. Or only your lips, even. I'd take your spider lashes, and be happy, really. Don't understand how anyone thinks we look alike. We look nothing alike, you're all Mom, really, gorgeous Mom with the symmetrical everything, and here I am, lopsided, with these crazy knock knees. I can't stand them. Cy. Cy? When you get a chance, I want to go over the books, when you get the chance, we *got to go* over the books already, I told you, I keep telling you everyday, already, when you finish that damn piece, *let's get to it,* now, Cy. Your coffee's ready, and I'm not getting it."

The buzzer sounds, Emerald in the bathroom, Cy's eyes closed, foot pedaling, fingers hummingbird wings, and the buzzer sounds again.

"Cy? Get it! I'm on the toilet. Could you possibly?"

Emerald runs from the bathroom, hits Open for the door, she knows it's Tim, she runs back to the bathroom to flush, brush her teeth, dab a little Vaseline on her lashes, pinch her cheeks, open her eyes wide, check for veins, drop the stuff from Paris all the girls used when she was modeling but couldn't make it because she was a tad too short, at the time, a tad too ethnic or else not ethnic enough.

"Okay. Let's get it together, Princess, what's this? Not dressed yet? What time d'I tell you I'd be here, huh?" Tim says, his dyed-black coif preceding him as he pulls Emerald into him, licks her squared jaw, Cy squeezing his eyes, head splitting.

"Can't leave yet until we've gone over these books, I keep telling him, Tim, he won't talk to me this morning, really, and I'm not leaving until we get the books straight, and . . . "

"I'm not going in today." Fingers stop.

"What do you mean, not going in? It's Fri-day, Cy, we can't swing it just Burt and I, what do you mean?

"Not going in. Just *swing* it. I haven't had a Friday off *for a year,* and I'm not going in. Simple as that."

"You spoiled little motherfucker," Emerald says, heading for the coffee.

"Oh shit," Tim says, running after her. Too late, she's hurled the hot liquid on her brother.

"Hold on there, girl, you just simmer down there, Missy," Tim says grabbing her arm as Cy flings the liquid from his fingers to the floor, shakes like a dog, heads for the head, not looking at her once.

"Can't take this shit anymore, really," Emerald says, coffee pot still in hand, Tim holding onto her arms from behind. "He gets *everything* he wants, he walks around, everyone handing everything right over to him, really, and if that's not enough, he *finds money* on the street, you know, he walks down the street, finds $60 here, $60 there, and then $2000 in a *public bathroom,* for godsake, and men all over the place just *lining up to give him whatever he wants, lining up to back the bar,* or whatever in fact he wants, and Mom, *why even bother to discuss her,* when it comes to him, and then there's me, knocking my head against the wall, trying to scrap a buck, running this *godforsaken bar by myself,* really, and there's Cy, from the day he was born, just handed all to him on a goddamn baroque and golden *diamond in-laid* platter!"

"Simmer down, will you there girl? What is it with you two anyway? I wonder. Just what is it that would keep a grown girl living with her grown brother? What is this sick crap between you two anyway? I'm sick of it, now, Missy, you just get yourself cleaned up and let's get the fuck out of here. I'm *hungry.*"

"Cy?" Emerald yanks herself away from Tim, puts her lips to the bathroom door. "Cy, get out of there already, will you? Come out here and talk to me, will you? You haven't spoken to me, really, *in weeks.* I'm sorry, okay? But you're getting to me already, there, Cy. Cy?"

"Well, girl, if you don't get yourself cleaned up right now, there Missy, I'm leaving. I need some pancakes and some eggs right now, and I'm sick of all this sick *shit* with your brother, all right? Are you sleeping with me, or are you sleeping with him?" Tim breathes hard, his forehead pale white and shining with a pimple, his top pink pink lip fluttering.

"Cy?"

"How old are you anyway, girl? If you start crying now, I've had it with you, I'm telling you. Are you coming or not?"

"Do I look dressed to you!" Emerald's head snaps around, Exorcist-like. Door still closed to her, shower goes on.

"Baby," Tim says softly now, holding onto her again, rubbing into her bare behind with the cold buckle clasped over his jeans. "Baby girl, get your head together now, okay, Princess? Your brother's cleaning up now, you drenched him in hot coffee, he's entitled to his shower, and tonight you'll be just fine with Burt, he's a big fellow, there, nothing will go wrong, and I'll even drop by tonight. So let's get out of here, now, Honey, what do you say?"

"Fuck off, Tim."

"Have it your way," he says, with his hands in the air, surrender-like, "just have it *your way.* I just don't understand what happened to that Japanese gene in you, Missy. The black is there, all right, here it is jerking us all around here and there, over your white one, but *where in the hell* is that Japanese gene, baby?"

Too late, the shower off now, the door bangs open, Cy wet and the towel hurling in front of him, Emerald out of his way, because she doesn't have to defend herself now. Never ever mention *Japanese* to Cy, although Emerald can *sometimes* take it, but don't mention it near Cy because it was the father they *never met,* much less knew, and he was only a trick, this Japanese guy, to their mother when she was in Hawaii, which was after St. Louis where she was born. But this Japanese trick was her lover for two babies, so he wasn't in fact a trick at all, but she refers to him always as the trick, *Your father the trick,* she used to say to them in New Mexico which was after Hawaii, and then in LA they were old enough to have an opinion of their own. By that time they were dealing with the black in them which is barely in view to anyone since their mother is half white and half black, the former overtaking the latter. Their blackness was never an issue to anyone looking who might call them, say, a younger, more tender version, male and female, of Yul Brenner. Still Cy takes issue with this father, this Japanese father, whom he tried to reach very very much in vain.

Tim on the floor, Cy's chest pulsating, Emerald does nothing since she would have done this if Cy wasn't first and utmost on her mind. Tim is a shiny shiny pale thing looking up with wide eyes at Emerald, as if this might extract an apology from her. Finally Emerald offers up her hand, since she decided against spitting upon him.

"Get your redneck ass out of here," Cy speaks first.

"Calm down now Cy, Tim you just give me your hand already, really, and I'll be dressed, and I'll take you down. Okay?"

"I'm not going in tonight, Emery, so get his comic book redneck ass out of here now."

"I should kick your ass right now, *faggot.*"

"Tim."

"That's what I should do, but out of respect for your sister, I'll walk out now, pretend this never happened," he says, letting go of Emerald and he's up, flicking his wrists as if there were bugs crawling on his hands. "I'll wait for you outside there, Emerald. Don't be too long." The door slams behind.

"Cy," she says softly, holding onto him as he approaches the piano. "Why do you have to go and mention the comic book thing, really? You know, it would be like putting down your music, or something. That's his *life,* you know, Cy. Be reasonable, after all. Here he is finally making something of his life, doing what he loves, being *paid to write* comic books, and you have to go and put it down. It's more than you could say for you and me, really. Look at this bar, where's it getting us with what we want, after all? Have you ever been paid, Cy, for your music? Have I ever been paid, Cy, for my clothes? Have . . . "

"Why do you think I'm not going into the bar tonight, Em-er-ald, huh? Just get out of here. I don't give a fuck about the books now, so just go, go on now to your Southern redneck dick."

"That's enough, now Cy. Give me a break, will you please, really? Tim never means it. He just got impatient. It's his way of joking, his way of jerking around."

Fingers hummingbird wings, Emerald turns her back to him and the piano, looks at the floor, the many scarves, silks, satins, swatches of linens on the floor, all the materials gathering together in her head, the colors swift and light as birds' wings, and they take off in flight. Her forehead smoothes, her palms together now as she blinks quickly, trying to call up the roof tearing off, but her brows furrow, Cy's music gets in her way, even though it is beautiful, it is Cy getting in her way, even though he is *very beautiful* and everything to her it seems to her at times, but he's getting in the way now of the roof coming off, tearing off, as she wants more than anything else for her problems to take to the sky, and she displaces this with missing a love in LA, missing another love, and then there are the streets she begins missing, her mother now moving in, the image of her hands brushing her ears, nervously the way she does, then turning her head because she didn't want Cy to move away from her, it isn't Emerald at all she ever misses, when she calls it's always Cy she asks for, *How is Cy doing?* her mother asks confidentially, as if Emerald would ever tell. Her mother thinking it their fault he's a manic-depressive, when who knows, it could have been *the trick* who gave it to him after all.

"Cy? Talk to me, please."

The door is banging, since they forgot about Tim.

"Hold on there, will you, Tim!? I'll be ready in minutes! . . . Cy?"

From the floor, Emerald picks up a large yellow scarf with

black Aztec-like lines running through it. She ties it around her waist for a skirt, then finds her shoes in the small defined kitchen. Her bracelet is on the piano, and she leans there, watching hummingbird fingers, then she looks at his closed eyes, the spider lashes fluttering, she touches his hair shaved close to his head, the mole near his eye, above the top of his cheekbone, he breathes in, and she listens to his feet on the pedals, she touches his neck still wet from the shower.

"Cy? It's okay, you need a break from the bar. It'll be fine, Burt and I will be fine, don't worry." Emerald smiles to him, hoping he'll look but he never opens his eyes. Suddenly it occurs to her there is something altogether different in his air. The thing she reacted to at first, his spoiled nature, seemed the usual, as the usual jumping into his bed every morning to wake him like a cat. But he seems different, at peace, even though he knocked Tim to the floor, and his anger did make her feel better, but then this *peacefulness* of not talking to her really, not looking at her as he often doesn't, still seems altogether different in this air.

"Cy?" she whispers.

"Yes, go on now."

"Okay. Don't forget the pills, will you, Grandma?"

"Yes, go on." Emerald stops for a moment because he didn't laugh.

"Grandma?"

"Go on."

"You won't forget the pills," her nostrils flare in concern. Cy opens his eyes.

"Get out of here, and go eat, before you throw anything else."

"Okay."

Emerald is at the door, now ajar, Tim tapping the first stair with his scuffed boots, she closes the door again, runs back to the piano, whispers. "Cy. I love you. Don't go tumbling down through it today, promise me? I'll kill you if you do something *stu-pid."*

Cy smiles, she kisses his nose, leaves finally.

Emerald takes with her the scent of coconut, Cy says to himself, his thoughts clipping his finger wings, and it's not like she's been around much anymore at all. There have been two, three, four even five mornings the past few weeks she hasn't been there in his bed like a cat, as always, that she hasn't been there with her nose, cool wet like a puppy, not there with her buds, warm, pointed and hard. Emerald keeps from him when she goes, days of rolling summer dirt New Mexico, like when they were young, rolling haze of hills, Emerald laughing, their mother running out, flicking her hands like a neon sign, and she'd say, *Let's surf some dirt, 'kay?* and they'd get up, catching dirt waves, arms flying, and they were truly trying to find the balance of the wave, on the hill, their mother kicking the dirt, kicking it flying, until they were screaming in laughter, yelling, *Dirt's up, dudes,* until they'd fall right on top of each other. No more holding his stomach in pain from too much laughter, no one would know he'd spent so much time like that as a child. Cy's been lonely, so lonely, no one knows what it feels like, to get up and fall back down in bed because you didn't want to see artificial light much less sun.

Cy gets up to Emerald's corner, as they call it, and it's no corner, but inches really where the sewing machine lies, Cy follows the curves there with his fingers, thinking of the coldness of bathrooms, Cy follows the innuendoes of the machine thinking of lips in his ears, wet, words stitching themselves into him like falsies of love. They are only tricks, Cy says to himself, eyeing the buckle, tricks like fathers, he says pulling it off the chair, quick as flies, quick as a whipping, he says, hitting it, zipping down like this, quick as falling, quick, look at it, quick as licking, and jerking, there, just *Think of me now, Emery,* quick as fucking, and it goes now, and it's all by and by, the way it coils into him, the pain, the way the disease takes him, the misery, the way *it can't be explained* to anyone unless you know it firsthand. The way you think anything coming out of you, anything coming from you, anything in the world you have in you, is just no good at all. The way you think the sum of your parts is still lesser, your whole being all the more worthless than that.

Cy holds onto the chair, from the floor, he holds onto the foldup in front of the sewing machine, with the belt next to him. *Take your pills, Grandma,* he says to himself, and he laughs upon entering the song. He doesn't need his fingers to hear it, of course, there it is quite plainly in his head, the beautiful song, he's only got half a chance in hell when he's playing, and nevermind his mother, he says, *Nevermind you, because you fucked it up.* I could never be him, and I hated him, you know that, and it just couldn't matter how much you tried blowing me up. Out of proportion you blew me, Mother, you tortured poor Emery, that way, you did, the way she goes on and on trying to please, *Incessant pleasure,* she once said to me plainly, as if she could make this all go away, as if she could step inside my head, squeeze the pain right out of it, as if she could step into my heart with her coconut smell, step in with her warm, cool lips, coax it like that right out of me, like a song. No, you made it impossible you did, for her, Mother, and it was always too late for me, as it was. *I can't take it anymore,* I just can't, what can I do now here?, nothing means anything to me anymore, Emery, not even pretending I can help make it all right for you, as you go on dizzily, as you keep right on thinking there's a reason for all of this, *misery,* isn't that what it is? right here in this place, no matter where on this planet we are? I ask you plainly how can I go on, in your life, helping just fuck it up? I'll never love anyone as much as you, I'll never love anyone, really, at all. I'm sick of this life, I could never share with anyone, no man anywhere with the patience to get any other, much less me, sick and fucked up here like a dog. I can't take it, I know, I'm sick and fucked up here like a dog. *I could kill him.* He did it to me, *that Japanese dog, Emery, he did it to us,* but it's not too late for you, like it is for me, because you can't know what it feels like, you just can't know, my sweet Emery Bored, what it's like to never want to get up.

He had had it all planned this Friday. Taking the chair here, beneath the sprinkler pipe, the rope like he has it, tying it like this, now it's done. All to do is just jump off the chair, nothing to it, Cy, is there? Just do it, thinking of nothing, father smile, and *fly on . . .*

Fall is in a hurry this end of August, Emerald's thinking as they make their way down St. Marks.

"Haven't I told you how I felt there, Princess? When I first saw you, wasn't I there with my feelings," he snaps, "just like that?" Tim gestures to the street as if presenting a garden to her, Emerald looks at it, then at his shoes, tracing with her eyes the surfacing of the bumps.

"I can't go with you, anywhere, Tim, much less to 'Bama, as you call it, how could I leave the bar for some place like that?"

"Because I want you to meet *my Mama,* Darling, what's your problem anyway with this bar? Let Cy get off his ass, for once, there you go giving him everything in the world he wants. You said it yourself, there Missy, and what kind of guy stands and takes the kind of shit, as I have there, with two sickies like you? *How could you question me?*—the kind of guy who indulges two sick cases there, like that?" Tim sticks his hands in his back pockets, squints his eyes at the cloud who's hiding the rays seconds before twilight.

"Please, Tim, give me a break already, really. If I was going to up and leave the bar, it wouldn't be to meet your Mama, or mine. It would be to take a trip, get the hell out of this dump of a city—*oh how I'm getting to just hate it*—here I am slaving over this bar, you see, here I'm just chained to the bar, really, with no help whatsoever from Mars." Emerald stops at a table of books near Astor, Tim picks up a comic book, scowls, throws it back down.

"Let's go now, Emerald, I thought you were in a hurry to get back home before you got to the bar. And what about that Mars, baby girl, you never know, hell, you might find your help up there—just climb on board this space ship," he says bending his knees, moving his arms in a chugging motion, "Get on here, girl, I was missing you last night, did you hear me? Missing you *so much.*"

"I hate street scenes, Tim, get away from me now."

"Oh come on, there, Missy. Don't you remember—what's it now? Eight months?—don't you remember, me seeing you there? And then the ad, the next week, and you saw it! Didn't it mean something there like that? Destiny, baby girl, all I have to say is, it was destiny, my words—'Wanting Girlfriend with the Pink Hair.' " Tim folds his arms, flashing a bright smile at the back of Emerald's head, as she screws the key inside the door.

"Did you think of it, Tim, if I'd changed my hair color? What would we have done?" she turns back, smiles blankly at him with her eyes glazing over.

"Who cares, Emerald baby? Your hair's still pink, but what if it weren't? You think that makes any difference to me, baby girl, if it weren't?" He climbs the steps, watching her, the olive arms swinging, the nice behind moving side to side.

"Can't hear that damn piano of your brother's, you notice that? He's going to apologize this time, when we go in. And I'll forgive him. He's your brother—albeit fucked up—but he certainly deserves a second chance. Like I did, really, with you baby girl. Who could have asked for a better beginning, a more romantic beginning, than us, huh Princess? Who could ask for better? Like I said, I'll even come by the bar, there, and help you tonight."

Too late, she opens the doors, the senses flying from her, like her breath, she falls backwards, Tim missing her in the volume from his mouth, Emerald seeing her reflection, there hanging, no life. It is *her life* hanging there, Cy, as she beats the floor, the scarves protecting, beats the body with her hands, the skin turning with her heat, it is *her life*. Someone tries pulling it from her, physically, limb from limb, she could feel herself tearing, she could feel herself bursting as she tries with her head. She could tear the floor from beneath them, she could fall too, from the earth, she could tear the roof and the floor from under them, so it would be over, and she'd find Cy there underneath somewhere, she'd find him underneath the scars, lying there spread eagle, it would be his face there scrunched up by the pillow, and it would be his smell laughing, *always,* it would be Cy and her together, together just like that.

Northern
California

Nepenthe

I watch the jet trails, hornets' nests under the overpasses, snow on the Grapevine, first time I've ever seen. Nepenthe drives wild, though her temperament never more than 20 m.p.h. I turn to look at her, sometimes snap her picture in between capturing clouds hanging low in the mountains, in the crevices that look like snow-covered vaginas (pussies). We enter a cloud now, a soothing white mist, we are riding it, then just as fast, we are in the clear. Nepenthe steps on the gas, cranks up the music, drives with one hand on the wheel, one hand moving across our space like the boys who use to dance with their own reflection at the Odyssey. She is trying to make me laugh. She keeps it up. I am laughing.

We are in love with the same man. That's how we know each other. But she is so young. She turned 19 yesterday

when we were in LA, now we're going to Berkeley to come to
some agreement. No we're not. This isn't a planned vacation.

Nepenthe is named for the restaurant—it means "no
sorrow" in Greek—her parents conceived her in the women's
bathroom. That's what she says anyway, and she's so proud
of the story. Her father is black, her mother white, her icy
cream coloring is warm. Her hair is dyed black, lots of hair,
very big hair, and she wears a tiny gold ring in her nose. There
is a tattoo of an ankh on the plush of her arm, just below her
shoulder. There is her body, lean but rounded with muscle.

We're coming up on the close dullish pink, blue, and
other colorless houses—we must be minutes from Oakland—
Nepenthe gets in the lane under the sign, Walnut Creek.

"Hey, and *suss* me out," Nepenthe sings with Marley. She
hasn't been saying much of anything, and as we're off the
highway it's dark and I'm wondering what I'm doing here. I
think of Clive coming out of the water, looking half his size,
how he dragged me down in the sand, still wet, the grains
sticking to us; when we moved there was that small, sharp
pain. I look at Nepenthe as she turns the corner—I hate her
beauty. She looks at me and knows it.

Her sister's apartment is so bare I feel suffocated the instant
we walk in. Nepenthe is carrying the cooler we brought, so I
hold the door open for her. I can tell she is sorry she's with
me. It hurts to feel those mutual moments of regret.

"Let me see if I can get this heater to work," she says,
rubbing her hands together. I wander off, look into the
bedroom of what must be her sister's roommate. The mattress
is on the floor, there is a chemical engineering book at the
foot of the bed, pictures taped tackily to the closet door,
almost everyone in the pictures is Korean. I hear the heat pull

in, Nepenthe dragging something from one end of the room to the other. I go to see if I can help her.

"What year is your sister?" I ask her, helping her pull the dresser over a yard. I have no idea why she is rearranging her sister's room like this.

"Fourth. This is her last semester, or so she says." Unsatisfied, Nepenthe is looking at the dresser. She rubs her hands together again.

"What sign is she?"

Nepenthe looks up at the wall near the ceiling.

"Sagittarius." She looks at me with a smile that says, This is irrelevant.

There is a bulletin board over the bed, pictures of her sister, many of Nepenthe and a few of their mother. Her sister is white—their mother's second husband is her father— and she looks nothing whatsoever like Nepenthe. Her name is unexciting, but spelled differently—Sherrel. Their mother has a very tight smile, holding onto the dog as if he might run away.

"Are you hungry, or what?" she asks.

"Sure, I could eat."

"Well, we could go into town, get a bite there, or we could see what they've got in their kitchen."

"Let's go into town." Fresh air would do us good, though I dread getting back in the car.

"Okay. Just let me pee," she says, unzipping her jeans, walking to the bathroom. I hear it come out, a strong, steady stream. She flushes, I figure I should go too. I enter the bathroom, she is standing in front of the mirror and she smiles at me. We look at each other's reflection, I stand behind her. What did he see in me? What doesn't he now see in her? She is too young.

Walking down Telegraph Avenue, Nepenthe stops at a head shop.

"We'd better get some candles and incense if we're going to stand the smell there tonight," she says.

I nod, but take this personally. I know I'm being ridiculous. There have been so many letters between us. Compassion for one another.

Nepenthe picks up some exotic oil—I imagine Clive spreading it all over her luscious body and feel as if I might throw up. Out of jealousy for him?

I pull out my wallet, she pushes it away. I don't know where she gets her money from, she doesn't work, her mother is not rich. The cashier admires the charms hanging from Nepenthe's leather jacket, she smiles at her and I want to burn out the cashier's eyes.

We eat at the same Mexican restaurant I've eaten at many times before. Beautiful tiles in the tables, I zone staring at the colors, waiting for our beers. It's chilly outside. Nepenthe pulls out a cigarette, motions to me if I'd like one. I take one even though it's been a year and a half.

"Those mountains looked really incredible, didn't they? On the Grapevine, the snow, I mean. I bet you got some great pictures," she says, so cheerfully, fake.

"Yeah."

"Maybe we should take the 1 back, don't you think?" she asks in the same merry voice, believing it now. She is different, like she has decided something and won't let me in on it.

She blows the smoke up high and to one side, then looks to see that she hasn't bothered anyone. The waiter brings our food, he watches her face as he puts the plates down. When she looks up to thank him, he smiles like he's melting.

"What would you like to do tonight? A club, a movie?" she asks.

"I don't really care if we do anything. I mean, we could just buy some wine and play Scrabble or something. Does your sister have Scrabble?"

"I don't know. We could look," she says smiling. She makes me feel so goddamn inferior. It's almost condescending, the way she talks. Her fucking smile.

I buy the wine—three bottles of it—I hope it's good, because I plan on drinking it all. Nepenthe opens the door to the apartment, I think I see a rat run down the hall. Nepenthe turns to look at me as if I'd shocked her. She scares me. She is reading my mind, and up until now has expected everything I've been thinking.

She turns on the boom box in the corner, switching the stations quickly until she finds her groove. I'm already on my second glass. She is looking all over for the Scrabble. I look at her ass when she bends over and wonder if this isn't desire.

Nepenthe kneels on the bed next to me, her face so close I can smell her breath. She is showing me a picture of her father.

"I can't believe this is here. Sherrel and I didn't know him really. I mean I was 11 when he left, and she must have been 8, but she wasn't even living with us. She was living with her father.

"He's very handsome," I say awkwardly.

"Yeah."

She gets up, puts the picture away, stands in the corner, stretches, yawns, looks around the room for wings. I feel as if her energy, which seems to have sprung out of a thin weariness, is going to boil up the room. I get tense watching her, until she turns around. Her back to me, I open my mouth to say something, but she cuts me off.

"I brought some hash. Are you into it?"

"Sure," I say.

She lights up quickly. I watch the smoke thick in the air. When I am so high, so drunk I don't know where I am, she turns on the electric blanket, so our butts are hot. She is giggling in beautiful ringing sounds. She starts singing the same line from a song. We're doubling back on the bed, bouncing back up, as she mimics a scratched cd. There are the two small candles with a quiet scent, flickering, the incense I can barely make out. But here she is, so close to me, intoxicating.

We wake up at one in the afternoon—maybe Nepenthe has been up for a while, she is lying with her head propped up, watching some soap. Her eyes tired, her shoulders shine. We are both naked. And I panic as if it were not me last night. How am I supposed to act? She seems bored and cool.

"You hungry?" she asks me, still looking at the TV. I'm fucked up, my head banging inside, but my body so warm in this electric blanket, next to her, I feel I'd die first before I get out of this bed.

"What did you say?"

"Are you hungry?"

"No, not really. My head is killing." I look at the TV, wait to disappear.

"I called Clive this morning," she says suddenly.

"You what?"

"I called Clive. I don't know why really. I guess I wanted

to wish him Happy New Year. You know."

"What did he say?" I ask her, sitting up.

"Nothing really. He's used to my confusion. Nothing really shakes him up, you know?" Nepenthe looks down at herself.

I start to hear what they're saying on TV. Absurd words. Nepenthe looks like she might cry and I want to slap her.

"Why can't you leave him alone? He's never known what he wants. He'll never know what he wants."

She leans into me, I hold her anyway. She is incredibly soft, and she smells like the musky oil we must have put on.

Nepenthe drives into the city, we go to the Haight. So hungry I can't stand it, we enter the nearest cafe. There are people here as shiny new as Nepenthe. She keeps looking down at the table, biting her lip. We order hot chocolates, wait for the omelets in silence. It's raining outside, people walking by look wet and beautiful. Today there is something I like about everything.

"Maybe we can look for a bikini after this," Nepenthe says smiling. Her nose is a little red, I wonder if the hole is irritated. I dare not ask her.

"Sure, we can go look for a bikini in this incredibly cold weather. Sounds wonderful," I say laughing.

We buy this little barrette with Coochie dolls on it—something like "coochie," they are Guatemalan—and Nepenthe sticks it in her purse. I've never seen her wear a barrette. But then I haven't seen her very much. Maybe 10 times.

"I like this bar," she says, as we get to the corner.

"This one?"

"Yeah."

It has the most smotheringly pretentious vibe.

Sipping on a gin fizz, she takes the excuse to come alive.

"Why are you always tripping on my age?" she asks me suddenly.

"What do you mean?"

"Everything you say. You looked at the waitress as if she'd card me. You're always saying something about me being so young. I mean how the fuck old are you?"

"Thirty two."

"Yeah. So what's the big deal?"

"I'm a whole *thirteen* years older than you. We don't have the same reference library."

"*Thirteen* years? Who told you that?"

"Those people at your party."

"Well I'm not nineteen. They were kidding. God, just a joke. What the hell difference does it make anyway?"

She is sitting on the edge of her seat, her anger not serious, full of life.

"I'm 25, you twit," she says.

I don't believe her.

"I'm 25."

I start to laugh, she stares at me with the straw between her lips until she is laughing too. A dude walks up to us, asks if he could buy us another drink. She is laughing really hard now, and as I come to the tail end of it, I look up at him, seeing Clive, so I fucking *hate* him.

"Leave us alone."

Nepenthe stops laughing, looks at me deadpan, gets up to walk out.

I follow her at about eight paces behind, she is holding onto her bag tightly, looking down at the sidewalk. Four or five blocks down, I follow her into a pet store. The owner sits above our heads on the steps. She bends down into the aquarium, staring at the reptiles. She wipes her forehead as if sweating. There is a chameleon with eyes like two fists working independently of each other. He looks at me, then back at her, and I'm feeling defeated. That she is not as young as I thought, shouldn't be such a big deal. I just thought she had to have so much more unspoiled than me for him to have left me for her. I don't know what the fucking difference is. I am too jealous, and want to own her.

Driving down the 1 we go through this rain cloud, then sudden bright sun. Nepenthe puts on her shades, contained, shut in. Her skin glows, hot ice cream, milk burning. Clive used to carefully place cookie dough on the sheet, size and order, everything according to plan.

Coming up on Big Sur, Nepenthe switches the tape. She hugs the soft shoulder of the road. What would it feel like if she lost control. What will it be like, sober, in daylight, watching her face when she cums.

"We can eat at Nepenthe," I say to her smiling. She looks at me, at first sadly, and then she warms up.

We walk into the restaurant, I give them my name because she is embarrassed. The hostess looks at her with fish eyes bulging out with enthusiasm.

Nepenthe tells me she has to go to the bathroom, and I do too. I follow her, she seems annoyed—I can tell by the tight quickness of her step—but, I'm going anyway. She opens the door to the bright pink, gold, green and blue, flowerchild sort of design of the bathroom. She looks in the mirror, I look at her from behind. I take her in my arms and kiss her.

"We can spend the night in Cambria at the motel with fireplaces you turn on with a switch," she says, her breath in my face.

"That would be good," I say, letting go of her.

She enters the stall, and I listen to the stream of her piss. Strong and steady, I could lie down beneath it.

"Yes, that would be heaven."

The Profit in Fort Bragg

Eustace has a shadow on his lung. His fiancée, Gita, along with her oldest friend Arielle, drives him straight from the doctor's office, three hours north of San Francisco to Gualala for fresh air.

Arielle spooks the view. Now half her body thrown out of the window, her butt moves in and out of the passenger's seat. Against the wind's whip she defiantly shakes her blonde curls. Eustace lies in back, knees up, feet on the armrest. Shadows of passing redwood tree branches snake his tinted cinnamon face. It makes his pain ring to think the women are death-free.

"Pull over here!" demands Arielle.

Gita speeds up, pretending she missed her chance. Arielle bops her on her bony knee.

"Those were seals down there!" squeals Arielle. "I wanted to see the seals. Hey, Mr. Peanut Butter man, didn't you want to see the seals?"

"Sure," he says, closing his eyes, "I wanted to see the seals."

"Should I turn back?" Gita flicks her tobacco-toned hand over finely waved kinks cut close to her head. Hoping to catch his eye, she peers at Eustace in the rearview mirror.

"You'd never turn around anyway, so why ask?" Arielle relaxes back in her seat, folds her arms, sighs.

Wild calla lilies grow off the side of the road. Eustace opens then squints his eyes so their gold tongues flicker with light. Waves splash up the cliff, then leave it foaming at the mouth. He imagines the waves sweeping up to swallow the car into the belly of the ocean. Eustace shivers, picks his sweater up from the floor and lays it over his chest like a blanket.

"You want the window up?" calls Gita.

"No!"

"You couldn't drive much faster," Arielle says, switching radio stations.

"Turn your voice *and* the radio *down* a couple decibels, will ya?" Gita snaps her finger twice in Arielle's ear. Arielle snaps twice back.

Eustace peers up at the sky. He sees buzzards circling overhead. Gita suddenly swerves to avoid the dead deer in the road. Eustace laughs, mocking a madman.

Arielle covers her ears, then rubs the side of her face, the peach fuzz on her cheeks like cashmere. She puckers her lips and eyebrows.

"I'm hungry," Eustace says, still laughing.

"How inappropriate!" answers Arielle, looking back at the deer, then at Eustace.

"We're almost there," Gita says.

"Yeah, but I'm *hungry.*"

"So stop here, Gites," Arielle says, pointing at the sign.

Gita pulls into the lot of the Old Meca Mexican Cafe. Arielle springs from the car, stretches her small, tight gymnast's body. Tall and lean Gita stands, holding the car seat back for Eustace, who very tiredly and over-dramatically drips himself down on the concrete. His face moist with sweat, his full lips shining, Gita takes his head in her hands. Imagining jellyfish, she kisses him, her taste buds like tentacles. Arielle walks ahead.

Waiting at the door for them to finish, Arielle pivots in her wrestling shoes, her ankles twisting. She waves her arms out like a plane, spins around, daydreaming herself out and away. Then suddenly from her left, seemingly out of nowhere, a young boy approaches. She sees he's carrying a black baby pit bull with light blue eyes.

"What's his name, sweet thing?" she asks, firmly stroking the puppy's head between his ears.

"Mine," the boy says. Maybe 12 or 13, his hair is long and greasy, his face curiously jailbait-sexy, his childlike chest covered in a too-large Charlie Manson T-shirt.

"I figured he's yours, but what's the baby's name?"

Slowly his eyes light up as if in recognition, then he cups the puppy's face in his hand.

"I said, *'Mine'.*" His smile grows slowly, a front tooth appearing to be chopped in half.

"How much you want for Mine, darling?"

"Much as you got," he says, his right hip swings out as he

shifts his weight.

"I got thirty. Will that do?"

He opens his hand, the fingernails filthy. He hands the puppy to Arielle, she looks into his eyes and he licks her chin.

"What the hell?" Eustace asks, Gita following.

The boy sticks the money in his back pocket, looks first at Eustace, then Gita, points and then laughs. As he walks off Gita watches, her thinly plucked eyebrows together.

"What in the hell are you going to do with a *pit bull,* Arielle?" Eustace asks, his hands awkwardly feminine on his hips. Gita holds Eustace's arm, then leans into Arielle to get a closer look.

"Just smell him," Arielle says. "Hmmmmn. I think I'm in love."

"Oh, for Chrissake," Eustace says, unlocking himself from Gita. His nostrils flare, then he heavily pushes the cafe door open, and disappears behind it.

"He *is* cute," Gita says, stroking the puppy's head. "But can you have pets in your building?"

"Who cares?"

"When are you going to learn, Ari? And how are we 'sposed to sneak him into the hotel?"

"They're separate cabins—totally private—you'll see. They won't notice us. Stop worrying. Go tend to your boyfriend. I'm not hungry, anyway." Arielle tiptoes to kiss Gita's cheek, then pushes her firmly toward the door.

The swollen and plush cushion of the red booth calls Gita. She plops down, listens to the swish of the vinyl as it sucks in her round bottom. Eustace holds his hands together over the closed menu. He won't look at her, a restless expression crossing his beautiful face.

The waitress favors Gita as she takes their order. Eustace slips down in his seat, fixates on the stomach beneath the pad and pencil, counting the lifts of her bulge with every breath. Hoping the waitress doesn't notice, Gita hits his knee. The menu falls from his lap to the floor. Gita bends to get it, hands it over sweetly to her.

He turns to watch the waitress move in pants that separate in many full folds, listening to the squishing sound of her thighs. Gita wrinkles her nose, and bops his knee again.

"Stop feeling so sorry for yourself. Stop being so mean," Gita says.

"Mean?"

"Yes, mean. Mean and short."

"Has it slipped your mind, Gita, that my grandfather died only last year of TB?"

"No, it hasn't. But you don't have TB, and you won't be getting it. You *had* a simple *pneumonia,* and the doctor said you've responded very well to the antibiotics. This has turned around. You'll kick it."

"Glad to know you're so confident."

"All of this sarcasm helps nobody."

"It's been *two* months, Gita, two months on and off these fucking meds, and you still believe it's a 'simple pneumonia.' Why don't you use your head, for a minute, huh?" he asks with wild eyes. When he sees fear in hers, he calms back down. "I'm just tired, Gita. So fucking tired."

"I know, honey. Look. Quit that damn job. That's where you got sick. You've done enough for mankind."

"Have I?"

"So all of this self-sacrifice is still noble to you? You want to work in a shelter for the rest of your life?"

"Don't start any shit with me today, Gita. I won't have you putting down every commitment I make."

"*Every* commitment? God, you constantly exaggerate."

"Oh come on. It's enough that Arielle is along, and now she's got a killer dog with her."

"He's a harmless puppy. What do you care? It'll keep her occupied. Let other people be happy sometimes, will you? My sympathy for you is running out."

"Is it now?"

Arielle enters cradling the puppy. Gita clasps her hands together on the table, looks up at her as if everything between them was perfect, and then she smiles.

"Give me the keys, Gite—I'll run and find some food and supplies for the dog, and be back before you're done," reading the scene, Arielle shoots a look at Eustace.

"Are you supposing that little hillbilly kept up on all the shots? That dog could be carrying *anything,*" he says, shuddering.

Ignoring him, Arielle holds her hand out, Gita pops the keys in, and she walks out.

"Lay off her," Gita says.

"Sometimes I wonder about you two."

"Do you, now?"

"Yeah. You're so damn protective of her. And tell me, why is it you never want to be alone with me anymore?"

The waitress brings their beers, he holds his up to toast.

"To all the black men dropping like flies," he says.

"And many happy returns," Gita clinks his bottle hard.

She cups herself around, nips him on the ear. She swallows

down half of her beer, wipes the foam from the corner of her mouth.

"I mean it, Gita."

"What?"

"Why haven't you wanted to be alone with me? It's been weeks."

"It has not. And I'm not going to argue with you."

"Hot plates," the waitress says, smiling again at Gita. "Very pretty necklace." Gita fingers it and smiles.

"Thank you," she says overly polite, waiting for her to leave.

Eustace twists the melting cheese around his fork, piles a mountain of rice, pushes it into his mouth.

"I wasn't going to say anything, but you know you shouldn't be drinking."

"Okay, we can pretend you didn't."

"*Eu*stace."

"One beer couldn't make things any worse."

"Fine."

"You're not really going to marry me, are you?" he says with big eyes, food in his mouth.

Gita gives him a weary look, then continues to eat in silence. They finish their meals without another word.

Arielle returns with the dog, a bag and the keys. She puckers her lips in a taut pout, announces she's taking a bus home.

"You are *not* leaving," Gita says, bringing the bottle down hard on the table.

"Sure, I am. I've decided. We're *in the way*. I'll just take Mine home, and get us settled. Eustace needs time alone with you. Anybody can see that."

Eustace inspects his pinky fingernail, then uses it to pick between his two bottom teeth. When he's done he carefully cleans it, and wipes both hands. Gita folds her arms in front of her, stares at her plate, then back at Arielle who is still standing there cradling the dog, the other hand clutching too hard at the bag. The puppy stares from Gita to Eustace then back again, his tiny tongue hanging out.

"Stay, Arielle. The more, the merrier," he says finally.

Arielle looks at the ceiling, then at Gita.

"Well, *I'm* not going to beg. I invited you because I want you here. You know that. You'll piss me off if you leave."

Arielle looks at Eustace, his arms are folded, and he's shaking his head from side to side. The waitress clears the table, leaving the check.

"Fine. Okay. So, let's go find this fucking 'St. Orifice' or whatever the hell it's called," Eustace says.

He gets up, leaves more bills on the table than needed, takes Arielle by the arm. Gita hangs back, picks up the extra ten dollar bill. He opens the door for them, turns around with a cavalier smile for the waitress.

For armpit air, Gita pulls at her blouse before she starts the car. Although Arielle spots the Russian architecture of the hotel, she lets Gita pass it before saying a word. She gives the puppy a perfect view from the window. When they double back, the yellow of the scotch broom dazzles at either side of the road. Llamas and sheep munch on the cold, wet grass.

With the key that Eustace had uncharacteristically dashed to fetch, they drive up the dirt road to their magnificent cabin on the hill. Arielle skips up the path, holding the puppy, sending loose pebbles flying behind her. She bangs on the door as if someone were home, and waits there for

Eustace to make it up the walk. He stops at the apple tree to pat its slender trunk. Gita wraps her scarf around her neck, focusing on the pile of wood on the porch. She closes her eyes, imagining smells of mustard, syrup, wine, as she hears Eustace jiggling the lock. Once inside, Arielle bounds the three steps in one jump to the bed, and lands on her back. The puppy jumps off, they hear his bark for the first time.

"You two can take the floor," she says laughing, spreading her arms out like angel's wings on the blanket. Eustace wanders around, staring at the woodwork and how it all connects. The puppy follows Eustace, sniffing at his feet. Gita makes her way toward the bathroom, pointing out the cot to Arielle who still lies with her arms spread out, her eyes shut in two delicate smiles.

"A Japanese tub! And look at the tile! Isn't it fabulous?" Gita calls.

"At $200 a night, it ought to be fabulous," replies Eustace, putting wood in the fireplace. The puppy still sticks close by.

Arielle descends the steps slowly, and stops in front of the bay window. Gita joins her, putting an arm around Arielle's stomach and the other around her neck, her hair spilling between Gita's fingers. They watch as the wind blows the apple blossoms, falling like snow from the tree. Squatting in front of the flames, Eustace watches as they grow, the heat licking his hands and his nose. The puppy barks, and he picks him up.

"I'm taking the dog out for a shit," he announces, looking at Gita and Arielle. They don't budge from the window. "Then, we'll go into town for some munchies," he clutches the puppy lovingly to him. Kisses him on the head, then with sudden paranoia wipes his own mouth with the back of his hand. He waits another moment for some response, but they barely acknowledge his absence as he shuts the door.

"So why the hell did you invite me to your seduction fest?"

"Seduction fest? Hardly. Well, why'd you come?"

"You *asked* me! I don't belong here in this love palace," Arielle says, dropping her hands from her back pockets. "Which is exactly what I thought the very first time I came here."

She sits on the floor, staring out the window at twilight. Gita watches her white skin glow, but it moves into gray when Arielle looks back at her.

"Just wanted you with me, is all. I miss you," Gita says.

"You're gonna mush on me?" Arielle cracks a smile.

"No. I just didn't want you alone moping. Forget about Tommy, already."

"I have!"

"You *haven't*. It's been months of distracted, aimless bullshit with you. Remember, *you* dumped him."

"And I shouldn't have?"

"No, it's best you did. But don't feel so sorry for yourself, either. In the end, you always get what you want," Gita says, drawing a map with her finger in the dull blades of the dark pink rug.

"And that is, at this point . . . ?"

"A new job, a new man. Daddy newly wrapped around your finger."

"That's not fair, Gita. What the hell is eating you? And why don't *you* set a date, already? You've been keeping him hanging for two years. Do you love the guy, or what?"

"What do you think?"

"I don't know, anymore. That's why I'm asking you."

"I'm tired of taking care of him. His life is taking care of strangers, and he leaves the rest up to me."

"He's been good to you, Gita. All of this time—what is it now—five years? Better than any man *I've* ever had, and you know it. He's sick, for Chrissake. Cut him some slack!"

"He's just about well. Anyway, he's *always* sick. He's a fucking hypochondriac. A neat freak, a germ freak. Obsessed with dying. Obsessed with imagining *all* of the possibilities of his death. I'm too young for this shit. I want to live!"

"Well, if that's really how you feel about it, you better let *him* know and quick," she says, getting up to snap her fingers near Gita's ear. "Don't keep him hanging like this."

"I can't leave him now that he's sick, Ari."

"You're beginning to piss me off, you just said . . . "

"I *know*. I mean, while he's still *convinced* he's sick."

"Whatever, Gite. It's your life."

Eustace pushes open the door, the puppy enters first, Eustace hiding his face with the bag.

"Mr. Peanut Butter Man! Wha'd ya bring us?" Arielle says, crinkling up her nose.

Eustace opens the armoire in the tiny kitchen, takes down three clean glasses. He raises them to the light, and although they sparkle, he rinses them. Arielle laughs, but Gita turns her gaze to the window. It is pitch black outside, and she cannot find the moon.

"Sköll," the three say together, as they clink their glasses full of red wine. Arielle rolls a joint, passes it to Gita, Eustace refuses, and Gita's relieved.

He takes out the extra blankets, pillows, pulls out the cot, makes a bed for the puppy on the floor, then one for himself. The girls chatter together, laugh. He lies on his side watching them, locks Gita's eyes with his until Arielle pulls them away with a cartwheel. Eustace, on his second glass, waves his hand back and forth in front of his face, mocking her, but then she does an aerial.

Gita giggles, the third joint burning the tip of her thumb until Eustace takes it from her to put it out. She crawls to his side of the floor, knocking over his glass, and he turns from her mouth. She lies him down on his stomach, sits on his ass, and rubs the back of his neck.

"Gita told me," he says, with a strained voice through the massage, "that when you slept over her house, back in junior high, that you never ate anything that didn't come from a can, bag or prepackaged box."

Arielle changes colors, her blue eyes fill so that the pupils are floating. Gita squeezes hard on the back of his neck.

"What's that supposed to mean?" Arielle hisses.

"Arielle was so into junk food then. All she ever did was eat potato chips. Eustace misunderstood me," Gita nervously waves her hand.

"And so what, Gite? Did your mom put some kind of shit in your head? Like I was instructed by my dad not to eat the food your mom made?"

"No! But it's not like he didn't want you spending the night in the flats, Ari. Wasn't until we moved up into the hills, that he was comfortable with your car parked outside our house," she returns, now angry.

"I can't believe we're revisiting this shit, Gita! Are we at Skyline again? Should I write another tome in your yearbook? And so *what else* did she tell you, Eustace?"

"Pardon me, girls. Nothing else," he says rolling over, as Gita has long since moved off him. "Would have loved to know you two girls back then," he mutters sarcastically to himself.

Eustace runs two fingers like legs across the floor, stops to do a can-can kick. The other hand joins, until Gita unfolds her arms, and slits her eyes at him, although no longer mad. Arielle takes an ice cube from her water glass, places it on his wrist, watches it melt down between the legs of his fingers. He flicks the drops at her face, sucks the rest, stops to examine the cleanliness of his fingernail. He turns to Gita, but she is heading for the bathroom.

Eustace smiles, reaches across the floor, juts Arielle in the chin. They look over at the puppy who's asleep. They smile at each other.

"You could never really start trouble between us," Arielle says to him.

"Oh yeah?" he teases.

"Yeah. We're thick as thieves. Just you wait and see."

"See what?"

"What's coming," she says with a smile, as she cups his cheek in her hand. "We need music," Arielle calls toward the bathroom, "I want to sing!"

Gita opens the door, gestures toward the toilet to emphasize the sound of the flush.

"She's so charming, isn't she?" Arielle jumps up the three steps in a single bound, grabs Gita from behind, locks her arms.

"Shush, the puppy's asleep," Gita says.

"Look at Mine, nothing would disturb him. I am so hiiiiiigh!" Arielle says, jumping down the steps with her eyes closed, then stretches her arms for the ceiling. Gita switches the box to a jazz station, sits down again on Eustace's butt.

Gita grabs his hand which flutters by her face, kisses the middle finger. Eustace turns around so she falls off, lands on Arielle's legs. Gita sits up between Arielle's legs, rests her back against her, takes another drag. Eustace pulls her roughly by the belt loop of her jeans, back toward him. He runs his tongue across her stomach, but she is already wet. Her head is in the spot of spilled red wine. She feels the long, blonde curls near her face, and lick-kisses on her eyelids. Fingers quicken at her waist, the T-shirt tugs at her breasts, chin, nose, then covers her eyes. All she hears is their collective breathing. Desire smothers. Her arms are locked above her head, her nipples hard between teeth and tongue. Like a ballerina, her feet point toward opposite walls. She gasps, her mouth baby-bird-open, and the tastes, the smells, familiar.

Arielle is wrapped in a blanket which Gita sticks one long leg out from under. Eustace doesn't remember who covered them there. He is in the cot, and also does not remember putting himself there. The puppy is nibbling at his bowl, looking up at him between bites. Just as Eustace decides he wants out, Mine looks up at him as if reading his mind.

At first Eustace doesn't bother to brush his teeth, or look in the mirror. He pulls on his clothes, gathers Mine in his arms, grabs the keys, and heads out the door. He lets Mine do his thing by the apple tree. But then Eustace slips in again, looks in the mirror, rubs toothpaste across his teeth and rubs it around with his tongue. He stands there waiting for the girls to stir, holding Mine under his arm. Since they don't, he finally leaves the cabin. Once Eustace turns the ignition, he thinks he feels Gita watching him, but there is no one at the curtains which appear unbothered.

He heads North.

Three hours later the light pours in, muted and grey. Gita and Arielle stir to the cold and mess of clothes surrounding. Eustace smiles from the open door. More light gushes in as he swings it fully open. Then he shuts it too loudly, and the room goes dark. He announces he has made an appointment for horseback riding in Fort Bragg. Looking neither of them in the eye, Arielle wraps her body in the blanket, then shuts the bathroom door behind her. Gita sits up, puts the cork on the last empty bottle of wine.

Eustace drops 100 bucks on Arielle's bag.

"What the hell *is that*, Eustace?"

"Arielle's profit."

"What do you mean?" she says, standing up naked. "That's not funny."

"I sold the puppy for $110," he interrupts. "Arielle made seventy, I kept ten for my trouble."

"I can't fucking *believe* you did that, Eustace. You had no right."

"No, *you* had no right."

"Me?"

"Yes, *you,*" he stumbles to the left, dizzy with anger. "And besides," he says trying to calm down, the taste in his mouth sickening, "Did *anybody* even ask me where Mine was? Did either of you, did *either of you fucking bitches,* ever, *ever* give a damn about that dog?"

It is drizzling. Arielle lies with her arms folded in the backseat of the car, Eustace drives. Gita's elbow hangs out the window on the passenger side. No one speaks, but Gita imagines the periwinkle whisper from the edge of the road.

Eustace peers at Arielle from the rearview window. She looks up at him, clears her throat, but she is hoarse from yelling. Eustace keeps looking back at her as if he could ever succeed in intimidation. Arielle shrugs and sighs softly. Gita looks at Eustace, and he back at her which is when he first notices that there is a lighter band of skin where the engagement ring should have been. He swallows and speeds up.

As he pulls into the lot he has already made up his mind to forget her, and Gita knows this.

In explanation of his accent, the guide tells them he is from Kenya. He is small, like Arielle, and dark with eyes like stars. While looking for a helmet to fit Gita's head, he says it will be difficult to remember their strange names. Gita tells him not to try, and to forget the helmet as well. Arielle wanders around the stable, stops to stroke the biggest stallion. The Swedish woman who is brushing down the first horse, spits in the hay before asking Arielle how many times she has rode. Then the woman disappears behind a stall, calls for the guide to bring her an axe. Arielle looks at Gita, Gita looks back. The guide returns with three raincoats, Gita takes the bright yellow, Arielle the dark green, and Eustace the same with a poncho and hood.

Gita's horse, with the burnt orange hair, pulls her to the side of the fence for water. They wait for the guide to mount the white one. Eustace takes his with ease across the dirt; Gita's gently sputters at the fence. Arielle, stretching her neck to look at Gita, focuses with trouble but Eustace interrupts her view with a slight and strange smile. Arielle subtly shakes her head with an unforgiving glance.

As they leave the ranch, the guide chatters with the effervescent lilt of his accent. Gita watches the road, the cars scaring her as they drive past. They leave splashes of tiny dots of mud on her pants legs. At the stoplight, she nods her head back to have a taste of the mist. Arielle waits again to catch Gita's eye, and when she does, Gita smiles. Arielle's brows lift.

They enter the woods, and Gita's horse follows the tail of Eustace's, tempting it to buck. When it does, showing a rumbling hiss of white teeth, Gita's horse backs up, pleased. Gita rubs her orange hair, then pulls the coat tighter around her own throat, feels the rain slide down her scalp to her neck. Eustace turns back, but she avoids his stare.

They are coming upon the water, Arielle behind, her chin bobbing in a dance with the move of her horse. She is changing colors—mayonnaise to grey to silver, beige to green to white—Gita feels a tug of old love for her. Arielle won't look.

A funny kind of calm moves across Gita's chest as her horse moves, with an angry glee, dangerously close to the cliff. Eustace's horse keeps turning around to make sure she is not in her kicking distance.

"Get 'em," Gita wants to say, but that would take too much effort. And it would spoil the peace as their horses ease down into the sand.

It is icy cold. The waves crash to a height Gita knows will soon obsess Eustace. He is faraway, and so another presence is made plainer to her as she looks toward her left. She doesn't see anyone. The guide has stopped his white horse so they can all look at the water. The line of the horizon won't show itself through the mist.

Gita moves forward, turns toward the rocks where she can barely make out the profile of a boy sitting with his head in his hands. Gita looks at everyone else, and they don't appear to notice. The guide still chatters away about the history of the place, Eustace seems to sink his mind into the water. Arielle is a transparent, brilliant pink. Her blue eyes are glassy, her yellow hair protectively grasping at her face.

Gita strokes the horse's back, whispers, kicks, and sends her galloping for the boy. The boy looks up right away as she approaches. His expression she can't translate, but she stops the horse at his feet, gets off, holds the stirrups for him, tells him fiercely to get on. When he does he looks at her, wiping his nose once, then nods his head back with a milky, inappropriate laugh.

"Go," Gita hisses at him.

When he takes off, she starts to run in the opposite direction, thinking everything predictable is now well behind her.

Mexico

Magda in Rosarito, Beached

"Cheek-lay?" the little girl asks, pushing with a small, thin, dirty brown arm across the table, running her fingers on the greasy formica, looking up at Magda and Tony with saucer-huge black eyes, her long brown hair falling in messy strands, escaping the green sweat band that holds what's left of a ponytail.

"You like chiclets, Mag?" Tony asks. Magda flips her hand like a fly buzzed her ear, blinks slowly, showing her hangover and a bit of her breasts in the torn Levi jacket she wears with nothing underneath.

"How much, kid?" he asks. The little girl bats her eyes at him, then looks at Magda to see if she has an effect.

"Get a couple, Tone. Maybe Deck wants some. We're out of gum, anyhow."

"Ready?" the waitress asks with a slight Mexican accent and jaded tone of voice. Magda picks up the menu, flips her bleached hair back, and puts a chiclet in her mouth.

"Not yet," Tony says. "How much money you got, Mag?"

Magda glares at him, then sticks her tongue through the gum so he can see it.

"Shit, Tony, are you *forever* the parasite." She motions for the waitress to return. "Get me a beer," Magda says, looking at the menu, "and some eggs, and . . . that's it."

"Scrambled?" the waitress asks. Magda nods.

"That's *it?*" Tony looks at Magda. "OK. Whatever . . . I'll have *this,*" Tony says, pointing to it. The waitress nods and walks off. "But no beans!" he calls after her. "Can't handle more beans, man. Shit has me fartin' every night."

"Yeah, yeah, Tony. Always the fuckin' gentleman."

"And ain't you ever the fuckin' lady, my *mag*-got. Heard you two all night, and then fuckin' ice droppin' on the bar floor above our heads. That room is so fuckin' cheap. And it smells like oil. Cold and slimy."

Magda's mouth drops open.

"I can't *believe* you, Tony. Just fuck off. You're such a prick. The *nerve* to talk about last night!" She glares at him long and hard. He blushes, and then as if with a newfound sense of pride and purpose, flushes the shame from his cheeks.

Magda dusts off her beer before the waitress returns with the one she ordered. Then she brushes off her thin, blue Indian skirt, jingling the bells of the draw-string waist.

"Hey, maybe Decker's with those dudes from San Mo."

"Yeah, maybe." Magda looks around, rolls her eyes, really

feeling the waste. "Fuck, Tone. I don't feel so hot."

"No fuckin' wonder, Mag. You haven't eaten *shit* all fuckin' week."

Magda flips her hand, then licks her lips.

"I know. I know."

"Doin' toot all night and drinkin' Bs all day—fuck—you party *too* hard, Mag. There *is* such a thing."

"Yeah, yeah."

The waitress brings the eggs and puts the plate down so hard it bucks before settling. She comes back with Tony's.

"Hot plate," she says as she walks off.

Magda takes a cigarette from her breast pocket, lights it, then blows the smoke in Tony's face. Tony smiles his straight-white-teeth-Pepsodent smile, then pushes back the two straight clumps of black hair from his pink forehead, and leans into the table to look at Magda. He stares into her eyes, then down her long pointed nose to the top of her white-frosted glossed lips, down her tan bronze neck, to the bit of breast peeking out. She opens the jacket up a bit more, the pink-beige skin peeling at her cleavage, and she laughs, blows more smoke in his face.

"I believe someone is *hungry,*" she says, still laughing until it sounds bitter and acid. A young boy enters the door with silver bracelets, shoving them in their faces.

"Ooooo," Magda coos. She takes a couple to try on. "Wha' da' ya think, Tone?"

"Hmph," Tony says. He looks away to put the fork in his food. The sun's hiding out. Looking way down the street, Tony watches tourists walking around in clusters, toting bags of Kahlua, silver, sarapes, turtle oil, beer, and beads.

Magda puts a five dollar bill in the boy's hand, then shakes her thin arm with its long blonde peach fuzz, so the bracelets clang in front of Tony's face.

"Pretty?" she teases with a mock stuck-up voice.

"Here comes Deck," Tony says. Magda's smile drops, she doesn't look up. She takes another swig of Corona, plays with the bracelets, then stares at her food.

"What's up?" Tony asks.

"Hey dude, you look cool. Really buffed," Decker says, grabbing a seat next to Magda. She looks up at him from the side of her clear eyes, then she hisses. Decker kisses her on the cheek, and puts his dark brown arm around her bony peeling shoulders. Tony smiles.

"Hey, did you see those dudes from San Mo, this morning?" Decker asks.

"No, I was totally out this morning. Magda lost it in the bathroom too, dude. It reeks in there."

"You OK, Babe?" Decker asks, squeezing her shoulders. She's looking away, playing with the fork of eggs, her cigarette burning, blowing smoke in the faces of people passing by.

"That dude Richie is *hot,* man," Decker says, taking a swig of Magda's Corona. "He hit the lip with a totally hot slash. Everyone was going whooooah—go baby!"

Magda spits her hack and the gum over the side of the table.

"Hey! You OK, Babe?" Decker asks again. Magda flips her hand. He catches it, kisses her fingers, licks the middle one slowly. Magda bops him lightly on his head with her wet hand which springs back with the bounce of his nappy orange hair, burned dry from the sun and salt water.

Magda smoothes her skirt down, and then opens her legs to put the skirt between them.

"Where's the truck, Deck?" Magda asks, her eyes looking sleepy, her voice hoarse and cracked.

"Up the street. It's cool," Decker says. He looks at Tony who has his chin in his hand.

"Thinking of pullin' out today?" Tony asks. He puts too much rice in his mouth, some falls out.

"Yeah."

"Where are the keys, Deck?" Magda asks.

"Hey? What-up, Chick? Chill out. You're uptight."

"Dad would kill me if something happened to his fuckin' truck."

"Yeah? Well nothin's gonna happen to his fuckin' truck. The dude has enough fuckin' cars to move an army, no-way."

Magda puts some cold eggs in her mouth, then spits them out. Tony has finished his rice.

"Get the check, already," Magda says to Tony. Tony whistles and the waitress comes out glaring at him harder than Magda does. She puts the check down so it whips the table.

"*What-Ev,*" Tony says to the waitress's back, rolling his top lip up so the gums show. "No one else has been this fuckin' rude. She isn't gettin' *shit* for a tip."

"I'll decide what she gets of *my* fuckin' money, Tone," Magda says. Decker gets up and stretches, then Tony does too. Magda digs in her breast pocket for the cash, sucks her teeth, and pulls out a ten dollar bill.

"That oughta be enough," Magda says, putting the money down, then holding out an open hand to Decker. Decker slaps the keys in it.

"Let's go," she says. Magda gets up, smoothes her skirt over her ass, walks in the wrong direction until Decker pulls her arm and turns her toward the right one.

"Got anymore blow?" Decker whispers in her ear, and she cringes her shoulders. "Woman are you on the rag, or what?"

"I *wish* I was on the rag," Magda hisses, then glares at him. Decker turns from her.

"Dude, you got the toot?" Decker asks.

"Nah, man. Magda dusted the shit this morning. I tell you dude, you better watch your chick, man. She's fucked up," Tony says. He spits on the sidewalk, and an old lady tourist sneers at him.

"Up yours, you old reppy," Tony says. The lady doesn't turn around. "So what's with all the reptiles in Rosarito this week, dude?" Tony asks.

"Who knows, man. This reppy slams on the brakes this morning, for no fuckin' reason other than he can't see shit. I had to swerve into the sidewalk, almost wasted a couple Mexican kids, man."

Magda opens up the truck door and gets in the driver's seat. She wipes her nose with the back of her hand and starts sniffling when she turns on the ignition.

"So yall wanna pull outta here now?" Decker asks.

"Yeah. If we make it before noon, check out time, we don't have to pay for tonight either," Tony says.

"No fuckin' *shit,* Tony, you dumbass. You aren't payin' for shit anyway," Magda says, backing up like a farmer in a tractor.

"Hey, watch the boards, Mag," Decker says with alarm. He starts playing with her hair then stops because he is too squished between her and Tony to keep the awkward position. Tony reaches across Decker and honks the horn.

"Will you mellow out, Tone! Like, who is the fucked up, uptight thing around here?" Magda says going the road, looking at both sides of the street at the baskets, ponchos, stone figures.

"You sound like such a fuckin' Val," Tony says, lighting up a cigarette he had rolled over his muscle in his T-shirt sleeve. Magda slams on the brakes and then pulls into the side on the dirt. She reaches across their laps and opens the door on Tony's side. He laughs, blows smoke, but then she looks straight at him.

"What the fuck are you doing, Mag?" Tony asks.

Magda pushes him hard with both hands, so that the cigarette flies out of his mouth as he lands on the ground.

"Close the door, Deck," she snaps. Decker does it. Then she pulls off. Tony gets up and dusts his ass, starts running after the truck but Magda floors it. The dust rises and covers all trace of Tony behind them.

"*Fuck,* Magda. All he did was call you a fuckin' Val, for Chrissakes. I mean, you are a fuckin' Val. What's the big fuckin' deal?"

"Just shut up," she says. Magda keeps driving, doing 80. "You closed the door when I told you, didn't you?"

"Well, yeah, but . . . "

"Then shut up!"

Magda is doing 90, and Decker puts both hands on the seat, gripping hard.

"MAGDA, slow up, will ya? You don't speed with a brother in your car, especially when it comes to the Mexican police. They could throw us in jail for the least fuckin' thing!"

Magda keeps jamming up the road, almost taking the

wrong turnaround to Ensenada, but remembers the motel is just past what seemed to her to be the last of civilization.

"So, where'd you go, Deck?" Magda asks, grinding her teeth. Decker, intimidated by the look on her face, takes his time.

"Told you. Went down to watch those dudes from San Mo."

"At four in the morning?"

"Yeah."

"Expect me to believe that?"

"Yeah."

"What about all the *'babes'* that were hanging with them, camping out in the grass near the motel?"

"What *about* them?"

"I didn't hear them get to sleep all night."

"Just as you mustn't have ever got to sleep all night."

"Look Deck, you had me up 'til four, or don't you remember?"

"Yeah, but who had you up past that?"

Magda pulls into the driveway of the motel with a wild swerve, swinging the truck so the boards crash in back.

"Fuck, Mag, the *boards!*"

"Tony did," Magda says, glaring at him as she pulls into a spot.

"Tony did what?"

She puts the emergency brake on, and turns off the ignition. Magda turns her face slowly to his.

"Tony had me 'up past that,' " she mocks with Decker's voice. "He found me in the bathroom pukin' and he helped me back to bed. Then he fucked me."

Magda gets out of the truck. Decker's mouth is wide open,

his lip just hanging there, as he sits in the truck. Magda walks on, her ass moving from side to side.

Decker finds her in the room, throwing the few clothes she has into the yellow duffel bag. Decker grabs her by the arm and squeezes, yanking her from her bent position.

"You're lyin', " Decker says, his teeth grit, his eyes red.

"No, I'm not."

Decker slaps her hard enough for her to land on the bed. Then he takes the keys from the broken dresser, and is out of the door. Magda rolls over on the bed, and takes a piece of lint from her tongue. Then she spits on the bed. She sits up, and looks around. From where she sits, she can see the cold, ice grey ocean out of the window. She closes her eyes, and rocks a little, but it seems like hours to her.

"What the fuck do you think you were doing back there?" Tony asks, standing in the doorway.

"Didn't Decker catch you on the way in here? How'd you get by him?" Magda asks, opening her eyes, no surprise nor malice in her voice.

Tony enters the room and stands in front of her, his white T-shirt with the "Rip and Tear" on the corner of his chest, a little dirty from his fall. He's red in the face, his narrow eyes piercing.

Magda starts laughing, cackling, then clapping her hands.

"What is so fuckin' funny?"

"You," she says in between breaths. "How'd you get here so fast?"

"I hitched."

"You must have just been dropped off the minute Deck was out of the driveway." Magda wipes her nose with the back of her hand.

"I don't think your shit is funny."

"Oh. He doesn't think my shit is funny," she taunts. She laughs again, her clear grey eyes half open in a witchy squint, as she rocks. One of her buttons loosens with her laughter, her pink nipple bouncing out every time she comes up.

"I told Deck you fucked me."

"You *what?*"

"I told him you fucked me this morning after he left."

"You what?"

"You heard me. You're supposed to be my friend, Tone. But you're fucked." Magda gets up and walks over to her small, olive green backpack. She unzips it, then clutches it in front of her crotch.

"Magda, you're fuckin' crazy. Deck is going to . . . "

"Kill you."

"You mean come back and kill *you.* He doesn't give a shit about your ass, anyway. Not a shit. I was your friend long before you met him."

"My friend," she mocks. "My *friend?* You mean you've been my friend ever since you found out who my father was. You don't give a shit, Tone, about me. You're just star-fuckin'." Magda digs into the smaller pocket of the backpack, grabs the small, thin black case, keeps it tight in her hand.

"What makes you think Deck isn't just star-fuckin'?"

"Because Deck *is* a star."

"In your dreams, Mag. Decker's no star anymore. You're sick. You're fucked up. With your old black, has-been surf punk, you think you have your shit together. And I've been your friend all this fuckin' time."

Magda jacks the knife out of the case and gets up to hold it to Tony's throat.

"Open your mouth, Tony," she says, digging in her breast pocket for change with the free hand. "Open your mouth, goddamn it, or I swear, I'll ram this in your neck."

Tony's brown eyes are bugging out at her, his skin a hot pink, his hands clammy as he opens and closes his fists.

"Magda, what the fuck?!"

"Do it, Tony. Do it! Open your mouth!"

Tony opens his mouth and Magda shoves the coins down his throat.

"Eat it, Tony! It's what you want, you fuck!"

Tony is choking, bent over, coughing the coins out, his eyes stinging from the metal and filth, his mouth running saliva all out on the floor. Magda takes the knife and slices into the back of his neck, as he's bent over, the blood spurts and runs.

He screams and grabs her legs. Magda kicks, knocks his head with her free fist, not letting go of the knife. Tony tries to grab her neck but she slices his hand, and she flees.

Magda runs out of the door, past the courtyard facing the ocean, past the bar, and finally the motel, until she's running on the dirt road, her thin, blue Indian skirt flying, whipping in the wind as she goes. Halfway down the road the spit works up her throat in that nasty way and she knows she has to throw up. She bends over, gets rid of the little nothing she has in her, the taste of stale beer nearly knocking her out.

She gets up again, runs. There aren't many cars that pass her since the motel is so far from town. Once she gets to the first stand, a little bakery, she stops and sits on the road, sees Decker hauling in the truck to get her. She lets herself be pulled in. By this time she's not sure what Decker's saying.

"I'm not even going to stop for your fuckin' things. We're

getting the fuck out of here. Leave Tony out on his ass."

In spite of his fury, Decker drives carefully. Magda is slumped down in her seat, her butt almost off the edge.

"You OK, Babe?" Decker asks, softening, turning back and forth from her to the road. Magda barely flips her hand, tries to work the spit for her tongue, but she's too dry.

"I couldn't find Tony. The fuckin' dick disappeared . . . Hey," Decker takes his eye off the road completely. "Magda-Babe," he says pulling over. "Magda?" he says turning her face in his hand. White goop in her eyes. "MAGDA!" he yells, shaking her. When she still doesn't stir, he stops, not knowing what to do next.

Los Angeles

What the Fertility Goddess Brought

Zen and Lourdes said there was always a sign on the trunk of the tree that said "New Orleans," "Monterey," or "25,000 Pesos to the Border." They never asked the old man if he was the one that put them there, but they knew he was. They'd pass him on the way back from the store; he sat on the front steps of the building on Gramercy Place, and Lourdes would say hello. He'd stare at her, his eyes looking wet with the black of his skin, the wrinkles in his face, the white beard and moustache growing into his mouth, like an Indian Raja. He would respond to Lourdes in Spanish, and she would laugh, grab onto the bag of groceries a little tighter, flip her hand dismissively when Zen asked what it was that he said.

Sometimes Raja would be outside with the baby, but most of the time not. When Zen said a child should never be left alone, the old man said the best way to screw up a child is to stick under its ass. He said his wife had done that to his son, and that's why he was dead now. He said the good-for-nothing mother of the baby was like spoiled, bleached Wonder Bread, and that's why she flew off to Berlin, or wherever the hell she went, and left the baby with his son. And that's why his son was dead. They said this all made perfect sense to him.

Zen and Lourdes had their hands full by the time they moved to Gramercy Place. It wasn't much better being just north of Hollywood Blvd., but Zen had finally gotten somewhere with the food technology degree and Lourdes had given in to her father, and so began managing the flower shop. There were no more of the all day lunches at Griffith Park, lying out under the sun and the trees, and wondering whether they'd get it together. But even with work, Zen offered to keep the baby every once in a while. Lourdes did not understand it, but she let him do it and she stayed out of the way. She worked later at the shop, and sometimes she'd go to her folks' place on Wilton, a loud lime-green house with tropical flowers growing as high as the roof. Then her father would ask her when she was going to give up the nigger and marry someone fit for her Mayan blood. And before Lourdes would leave, swearing she was never coming back, she would tell him where and how far he could shove it.

Vacation time came, and Lourdes was sick of Zen keeping the baby, complaining about IHOP and putting off a trip. She bought the tickets for the flight to Cancun so he could see her family's roots in the Yucatan peninsula. She said that Raja could watch their place and keep the plants alive. Zen agreed and said the baby liked their space and would enjoy staying there. He seemed to want to go for that reason.

Zen was useless by the time they'd taken the ferry to Isla Mujeres. Said he didn't like to lie on the beach, nor the way people stared at him. Zen and Lourdes would hang out eating shrimp, her eyes on the boats and his on the people, with his lip curled, his brows meeting off center. Lourdes said it was fine with her if they left, since he would probably like the ruins in Chichen Itza better. They took a second class bus full of Mexicans, and Zen complained that he couldn't stretch his legs, the children were staring, and the men were hostile. Lourdes cursed to herself in Spanish, and she let him fall asleep on her shoulder, as her neck cramped. He woke, startled by fires blazing in the jungle just off the road every few miles, then he'd hum himself back to sleep. She was sweaty and her hair was matting together, feeling stiff, dry, and thirsty; she hated Zen, and her father even more. The ashes came in through the window, and she thought about Raja and the plants.

Zen climbed the stone steps of the pyramid like an athlete in his prime, stopping only to look back at her as she pretended she wasn't scared. Birds flew out of the dark entrance like bats from a cave and when Lourdes screamed, Zen kissed her like the first time they'd met. When they got to the small cafe in the middle of the jungle, they bought Squirts to drink, and a fertility goddess for Raja. Zen packed and unpacked it, wrapping it four times over to make sure it was okay through the traveling. By the time they got to Merida, where Lourdes thought Zen would feel good in the city, they were both ready to go home. There were soldiers on every corner, even more by the cathedral near the Palacio Gobierno, and Lourdes tried to explain. But Zen wouldn't listen, said he missed the baby.

When they got home they found a bleached-haired, white girl lying unconscious on their living room floor. Lourdes screamed, said fast prayers in Spanish to herself, the tears and sweat breaking at once. Zen was quick on the phone, his lips in a straight line, his voice in control, with a strong hand on Lourdes' arms. She was crying when the ambulance came, and later when the police arrived. Zen went over the story again and again, how they did not know who she was, how they found her, nothing was broken in the place, they hadn't even unpacked, just back from the airport. He never mentioned Raja's having the key. Lourdes was staring at Zen's yellow pants, and she couldn't look at his face. The police left and Lourdes kept crying, staring at the carpet where the girl had been lying. Zen said nothing and slowly started to unpack. When he got to the fertility goddess, he said he'd better take it on over to Raja, and that it would make them both feel better if they saw the baby. Lourdes repeated she didn't want to go as they were walking out of the door and up the steps to Raja's place. Zen held her hand, smiled at her with his one dimple, and suddenly she remembered him the way he was four years before. When Raja opened the door, looking older than before they left, she felt everything tighten up. Then the baby started crying as they gave Raja the fertility goddess.

He didn't even say thank you. The first thing out of his mouth was, Is that white bitch in your apartment dead yet?

White Picket Fence

They are married lovers, still. Every afternoon Frank and
Ellen take a long walk down Crescent Heights to Melrose
Avenue, then up Fairfax and back to their duplex in an old
Jewish neighborhood, LA. Frank holds Ellen by her small,
blue-veined hand, leading her as she jaws to herself; she
tugging the tip of her blue baseball cap, down to the few hard
strands of brassy white on her wrinkled, freckled forehead.
Ellen is thin and walks with her head down, making sure her
legs are keeping her up. Frank is tall, with an Adam's apple at
the back of his neck. He wears grey slacks and Nikes; he has
all of his thick, light blue hair.

Frank likes pot roast and macaroni so he makes it three
times a week, eating the macaroni with a spoon from the
pot because it's always ready first. There at the table Ellen

sits, chewing on her tongue and the last of her jaw teeth, sometimes spitting out the food when he puts it in her mouth. Frank kisses her tenderly on the forehead when he takes the cap off her and she closes her eyes with a shiver, then a shudder. She puts a shaky hand on his shoulder and makes a gentle sucking sound with her tongue and the roof of her mouth.

When Frank has to go somewhere alone, carefully he takes Ellen downstairs, out to the front lawn. When he closes the gate of the white picket fence, she is right there behind it, staring at the make-shift lock, the wrinkles in her forehead moving deeper, closer together. Then she screams as he goes down the block. When he's out of her sight, her screams settle down to a hoarse holler, then she starts pacing the lawn back and forth, now jawing to herself quietly, until he gets back.

Why I Could Never
Be Boogie

Boogie and I meet after school 'round four to race the turtles, or ride our bikes to the liquor store and back. Boogie's a bit slower than me, which bothers him 'cause I'm a girl. And Boogie is so fat—I think he's no more than 10 and only a head above five feet, weighing up there in the two hundreds of pounds. Boogie is *huge*. But he's cool, shows me the hangs around Washington Blvd. and the Avenues—I just got to my Grandma's in LA, and there's nobody but her, and Boogie next door, to show me what to do.

'Round seven Boogie has to go inside to scratch his father's dandruff and oil his scalp. Boogie's old man has long, good, wavy, white hair—I think Boogie and his folks have a lot of white in 'em. Boogie is creamy colored with fleshy fat, which is fine, 'cause Boogie's still pretty. His father too, who sometimes lets me come in and watch as he sits on the floor under Boogie. He has long black eyelashes that he looks at you from behind in his sneaky sort of way. He pats my butt whenever I leave, and I turn around and smile because I know he means good. Other times I'm not allowed inside because Boogie's mother works. She's a nurse over at one of those fancy hospitals somewhere—I know it's fancy 'cause Boogie said the patients arrive in limousines! Imagine that. I even seen a fancy car pull up in front of Boogie's old rinky-dink, yellow house. I couldn't see who got out 'cause Grandma pushed me from the window. Don't know why she did that.

But Boogie and I, we're going through some lows, 'cause Boogie's getting shit 'bout his fat and his smell, and I'm getting the big-titty, big-booty shit at school. But Boogie and me, we've got the turtles, we got our bikes, the liquor store, and we've got each other. So today we ride our bikes to the store for some Now and Laters, but I have to go to the bathroom *bad.* Grandma's not home yet from cleaning the Birds' house in Bel Air (The Bel Air Birds, I call 'em) and I left my key at home before school this morning, and we can't go to Boogie's 'cause his mother's working. So we beg the liquor store owner if I can use the bathroom, and we try and explain the situation, me close to tears, and the man just keeps shaking his head no. I can't see Boogie 'cause my eyes are burning and I'm starting to cry, now the hot pee is stinging as it streams down my legs into a dusty, yellow puddle on that asshole's cracked floor. I feel sick, and Boogie's pulling me by the arm out of the place, and he's getting me on my bike. I ride home behind Boogie, sniffling, feeling hot and red as a beet, the piss drying to a thick stickiness between my thighs and legs, and on the inside of my sock.

Boogie's father answers the door with a "no-you-can't-come-in," because Boogie's mother's working. Now Boogie's throwing a tantrum, and yelling, "who gives a shit if she sees that old white bitch anyway!" I don't have a clue what Boogie's talking 'bout, but Boogie's father grabs him by the ear, clamps his mouth, and slaps him hard on his fat cheek. But the odd thing is that he pulls us in the house anyway, and I'm allowed to go to the bathroom to clean up.

The house feels dank and clammy inside, and I hear this muffled, retard-like voice coming from across the hall, so I peek, and there in the bedroom with the door half open is Boogie's mother in her nurse uniform, and a white woman with black eyes, blue cheeks, and bandages covering everything else on her face. The smell of medicine and the look on that battered woman's face sends me to terror, I can't help it, I scream. And now Boogie's shoving me into the bathroom, and he closes the door, hugs me up, me, smelling high with pee like that, and we stay there, me, still terrified, until Grandma comes to fetch me.

Grandma puts me in the bathtub at home, the soap smelling like lemons, and Grandma's hands, huge and soft with rough lines, splashing the bubbles over my body, 'til it soothes me to sleep. I wake to the smell of fried bananas, black-eyed peas and coconut rice. I hug Grandma from behind and ask her what's wrong with that white woman at Boogie's.

"She had a face-lift," Grandma says, and so I ask her what that is, and she says, "it's when doctors cut your face and then sew it up to look younger."

I say I thought the woman was hiding from thugs who beat her up. Grandma says, "You could say that too."

I'm completely confused, and Grandma's laughing and says, "She's just hiding while she heals up, and she wanted a place where nobody would see her. Boogie's mother's been keeping white women like her for years now. Extra money, you know."

I say to Grandma, "Wha' da' ya mean where *nobody* can see 'em? *I've* seen 'em, *Boogie's* seen 'em. Boogie's mother *and* father's seen 'em." Grandma just laughs.

I'm mad. That beat-up white woman gives me nightmares. And now Boogie and me stopped talking. I play by myself with the turtles, and ride my bike to the liquor store alone, where every time I look to see if my pee has left its mark anywhere on that asshole's dusty, cracked floor.

The Breaking of Miss and Mrs. Gaines

A sincere fuck, was what Anna told Jazz she wanted most from him. Then he could go since she didn't need him for anything more. She wanted to feel free. No more guilt, no more misconceptions, or obligations, just peace of mind.

Jazz was lying on his back, an arm stretched out, the hand as if it held a good book. The other arm thrown across his face, covering his eyes.

The sun was streaming in and as she stared at the sycamore tree in front of the window, the leaves poured in, floating up to the ceiling, circling around in a rush. The green was overwhelming, and she wanted another beer, or at least to finish the one she had half drank with breakfast alone that morning.

She touched his side and when he didn't move she got angry but tried not to show it. It was Sunday, and there was something she was supposed to be doing, but she couldn't remember what.

When he finally rolled over both arms were above his head. He looked like he could be floating dead on water. This didn't scare her. He had told her she had fire in the mind, and the way she thought burned her head. Maybe she would die in the ocean, she imagined; this would be the only way to put it out.

He moved to his side, opened one eye, looked at her as if recognizing. She smiled, closed her eyes, tried to feel the wind the leaves were making, rushing above their heads in a circle, even closer to the ceiling now.

"Anna, wake up," he said softly. "Anna, get up," he said, nudging her shoulder, throwing a leg across her body. He nuzzled up against her, put his nose in her hair, so that she would scratch him, make him itch, maybe make him sneeze, and they would laugh, and she would say she loved him, and he would be happy until they got out of bed.

"Jazz, get up," she said, her eyes still closed, the ache between her legs, her muscles tight, her arms heavy. "You'll be late, Jazz, get up."

He rolled out of bed, made a loud thump on the floor, and then groaned to make her laugh. But she didn't.

"Three months now, Jazz," she said, opening her eyes, looking up at the ceiling to see that the leaves were gone.

"I know," he said.

"I don't need this."

"I know."

"I don't want it," she said, shaking her head, holding a tight fist.

He was standing now, holding onto the dresser, facing the mirror. He opened a drawer slowly, then held his head like it hurt.

"Look what you did to me last night," he said, turning his face toward her, pointing at the purple under his eye.

She closed her eyes, tried thinking of all the things she had made by herself. An ice cream candle in sixth grade, a clay dragon in the eighth.

"Look what you did!" he shouted, coming closer to her.

And when he was in her face she grabbed his long dark hair, pulled his head back, and said real slow, "I - don't - need - you." When she let go of his hair he slapped her so she would cry. It was always good when he slapped her because she had held the cry for so long. She could let it all out, she could let it all go—show him she didn't need him. He wasn't the only one alone in the room.

When he held her, she would hum a little to herself as she cried. This made them both sleepy. This made them stay in bed much longer, on top of the sheets, where it was too warm to be under, too hot to be over.

Anna stopped her crying since the room was now on fire as she had wanted it. Jazz's nose was in her red, frizzy, wavy tangles; he was kissing her neck and the scoop of her collar bone, on her breast, around the half moon, and in the soft place where the kiss sinks in.

"I don't need you," she whispered.

◆ ◆ ◆

Mrs. Gaines thought it would be best to put the fishbowl out in the hallway. That way people could pass it by when they visited instead of having to stare at it as they sat in the living room, or worse yet, that she would have to stare at this bright orange fish with fins like flames, in her bedroom. She would never sleep. She got little enough as it was. But Anna had told her to get the fish, last time they spoke. Anna thought it might calm her down. Her daughter told her she had fire in the mind, Mrs. Gaines assumed this was why she never got to sleep. Mrs. Gaines put the picture of her dead husband face down every night before she got in bed. She told herself this spared him of any embarrassment he might have. Mrs. Gaines slept, whenever she did sleep, alone. But because this was enough for her, she decided it was embarrassing to him. But she really didn't need anyone.

Anna had left her a year ago for a willowy sailor named Jazz. Mrs. Gaines hadn't really believed he was a sailor, but this is what he'd said. She figured he was stupid enough to be in the navy, though he didn't look very strong. And then there was his too-long hair. Mrs. Gaines figured he was really just a rich surfer from La Jolla that could make things. He'd carved her the most beautiful chess set before he took Anna away. Then his beating her at chess told her he wasn't so very stupid. Perhaps he was only soft, a bit too bendable. Anna didn't need that. Anna had fierce will. Mrs. Gaines had given Anna her fire in the mind, after all.

Mrs. Gaines picked up the phone to call Anna. A recording announced that the phone had been disconnected. It's no wonder, Mrs. Gaines thought, because Anna never worked a day in her life, and Jazz's money couldn't last that long. Even if he really was a rich surfer, thought Mrs. Gaines. His hair was too long for the navy.

Mrs. Gaines put the phone down and contemplated the kitchen. She could put the fish on the counter, and it would discourage her from picking at the food as she made it. She was usually so proud of the food she made, but ashamed of the picking she did throughout the whole thing. She would put the fish in the kitchen.

The bowl was a little heavy to her, the water splashing up with the imbalance, the fish jerking around, afraid. She found the fish annoying, looking so paranoid. She thought, Why should a fish look so paranoid when a fish was so stupid after all? She wondered what kind of life a fish had, and whether it was fair or unfair to keep a fish in a bowl. She decided it wasn't worth worrying about since no one could tell her the truth. Things such as this shouldn't be worried about. Life was too short.

Mrs. Gaines turned her back to the fish, now on the long counter near the sink, and thought about what she was supposed to be doing. It was Sunday, but she couldn't remember. Didn't matter. Mrs. Gaines appreciated her own easygoing nature. She could take a nap. Slowly, Mrs. Gaines walked to the bedroom. This wasn't a day to be rushed. Things could be taken easy.

◆ ◆ ◆

Anna lay there with her legs wide open, singing to herself, and to Jazz if he was listening. He was lying on his side with his back to her, studying his fist. Anna kept singing.

"Get me a beer, Jazz," she said when she stopped, and as she moved she spilled his cum down the inside of her thigh. This was a relief to her. "Get me a beer, Jazz, now, please. I'm thirsty and tired and I want to go back to sleep."

Jazz didn't move.

"You're making things worse, just lying there. I don't know what you look like anymore," she said, pulling on his hair. "You never show me your face. It gets so I can see every fucking pore in your back. Please, Jazz, turn the fuck around."

Jazz stretched, opened and closed his fist, licked the bruised knuckles.

"Get me a beer!"

"When'd your mouth get so filthy?" Jazz asked, turning to look at her in disgust.

Anna jerked herself out of bed. She stood for a moment holding her head. When it didn't take off by itself, she started to walk. She walked slowly, in case Jazz had decided to get up. When she reached the doorway, saw it was futile, she crossed the threshold.

Jazz turned around to watch her leave. He imagined it was the last time he'd ever see her. This became reality to him for a few moments. It was good at first, then it was bad. He rolled over onto his stomach and buried his face to his ears in the pillow. It wasn't saying anything, so there was nothing to learn.

◆　◆　◆

Mrs. Gaines found it easier to sleep when she kept her mouth open and let the drool run free. She never did this when her husband was alive, better to keep sleep neat and decent. A little drool could be disgusting, she thought; a little drool kept the pillow wet. As if tears didn't.

Mrs. Gaines cried a little into her pillow when her husband was alive. She stopped when he died because she couldn't feel sorry for herself anymore. So she drooled a little instead now, somewhat happily, messily, never really sleeping too deeply, reaching it sometimes and snoring loudly. She imagined, snoring loud enough for her prayers to be answered.

Mrs. Gaines imagined she prayed when she slept, since she couldn't allow herself the concentration to pray when she was awake. But it was definitely something she believed in, there was definitely some One or some group of Ones or some Body or Force who answered the sleeping prayers. After all, her husband was dead, Wasn't he?

Mrs. Gaines smiled in her sleep, she imagined. She thought she must be beautiful when she was asleep. Her mouth a little open, drooling, and snoring and praying. Perhaps Jazz would take himself sailing, if she slept long enough. If only she could consciously pray and have her prayers be answered. It wasn't necessary that he die. Just that he go sailing or surfing or floating, somewhere else, away from her and Anna. And then Mrs. Gaines remembered that she herself would have to die eventually. She was wide awake now. The pillow dry, and the room quiet.

◆   ◆   ◆

Anna came in with the beer. She had a shirt on now, open, hanging off like it shouldn't be there, hanging off like she hated it but wore it simply to annoy herself. Jazz's face was still buried in the pillow, Anna hoped he was crying. When she came closer to him, pulled his long dark hair so that his head rose with his hands still grabbing the pillow, she saw he wasn't crying, and that angered her.

"I'll leave today," he said, as she let go of his hair.

"Are you taking the boat?" she asked.

"Yes. I have to get the hell out of here."

"Yes, me too," she said, looking out of the window, wanting the leaves to start pouring in again. I'm going with you, she said to herself.

◆　◆　◆

Mrs. Gaines suddenly felt her prayers were being answered, that Jazz was leaving and Anna would be back home to learn how to grow up properly, to learn how to control the fire. As she thought about this the more she became convinced, and this relaxed her to the point of considering bringing the fish into her bedroom, so that she could watch it swim and make the best of its situation.

Perhaps fish aren't so stupid, she thought, after all, they could just float in one place and then die, but they don't; they swim around and around and around.

"I'll move the fishbowl into the bedroom," Mrs. Gaines

said aloud, getting out of bed, and once she entered the hallway she found herself running to the kitchen, to the fishbowl.

◆   ◆   ◆

Anna and Jazz were lying in bed now, their faces pressed close together, eyes staring deeply into one another's, their arms clasped around one another's waists, their legs entangled.

"I'm going to have the baby," Anna said. "I wanna give birth at sea," she whispered.

Jazz said nothing, blankly staring at her face, thinking about what he had made.

"I think you're selfish, Anna," he said to her, as he turned from her embrace. "Much too selfish," he whispered to himself, his back to her. Jazz suddenly got out of bed. Anna watched him go into the bathroom, and shut the door behind him.

◆   ◆   ◆

Mrs. Gaines had the fishbowl in the bedroom now, and she didn't know why but after staring at the fish swimming around there on her dresser with its flaming fins, she started thinking about things of the past, and something made her feel just a bit sensuous, and then remembering a certain scene titillated her, and she started touching herself, and just a bit embarrassed she turned to see if her husband's picture was face down, and then feeling a bit daring she picked up the picture so that it faced her and then she lay back staring at the ceiling, then closing her eyes, she touched herself all over, abandoning more and more of her stipulations and confinements of the mind. This felt quite good as long as it lasted. But then it was over, and she got up and went into the bathroom to throw up.

◆　◆　◆

Once Anna heard the water running in the bath, she felt calm. She opened the door, Jazz was sitting in the tub. She could see his body, the water running over it. She climbed in and he made room for her. She lay back, facing him, and she closed her eyes. Feeling him there with the water running over their bodies was soothing. She could sail away with Jazz; she would go anywhere with him.

◆　◆　◆

Mrs. Gaines looked at the bathroom and felt satisfied with the job she'd done in cleaning the vomit, so she went into the bedroom feeling there was no need to be in the house. She decided that if the phone was disconnected at Anna's, she would just have to drive herself over and see what the trouble was about. Maybe Anna would come home with her. She knew there was trouble because the fish was so paranoid right then, even though the room was quiet and clean, and there was no evil. She figured the fish could sense some danger within her, and all that was within her was fear for Anna. Her daughter Anna. I'm her mother, after all, Mrs. Gaines thought. It took a long time for her to realize this. She had created Anna. She had made her, she was hers.

◆   ◆   ◆

Jazz put his head back in the tub, and it hit the candle Anna had made, still there from their last candlelit bath.

"When was the last time we did this?" Jazz asked her.

She was rolling her head from side to side as if there was music.

"Do you remember?" Jazz asked.

He moved his leg and put his foot in between hers, moving it up slowly. She kept her eyes closed and sang just a little. He ran his finger down the length of her leg under the water.

"Let's make love," Jazz said.

"Go to sleep," Anna answered, her eyes closed still.

"Let's make love, Anna."

"We are making love," she said. Jazz tried to move his legs as if they were stuck under hers. When he got tired of this, he knocked the candle onto the floor.

◆   ◆   ◆

Mrs. Gaines picked up the fishbowl. She turned around suddenly, splashing a little water, upsetting the fish more than it was already, because she saw the Bible sitting there on the dresser, all dusty, untouched. She thought, what a bad housekeeper I've been; the Bible shouldn't be so dusty. Maybe she'd dust it when she got back. After all, it was Sunday, a day to clean things.

◆   ◆   ◆

Sitting there in the tub, Jazz thought a moment about the mess. He looked at her lying in the tub across from him, with her eyes closed, her hair back from her soft face, her expression ethereal. All he felt now was pity for her and anger at himself. All she had wanted was to fuck, and he had gone on telling himself they were in love. Now he didn't want to hurt her. She was so young and very pregnant, he thought, looking at her belly in the water. Could water really be that distorting? He picked her hand up out of the water, to look at the wrinkles it had made.

◆   ◆   ◆

Mrs. Gaines was in the car now with the fishbowl in the backseat. She felt a little absurd taking it, but she reassured herself. She decided if she covered the fishbowl with a plastic baggie, with a rubber band tied around it, and a couple small holes for the air to get in, then the fish could swim in the bowl while she drove and it could experience a larger motion in the suspension she had made. It would feel the same bumps and sudden stops that she felt. The fish could finally go somewhere without leaving the safety of its confinement. After all, it was still in the bowl. The bowl was just in the car. And she thought if anything bad was to happen to the fish, it would be an omen. Omens were for warning. There had to be some sacrifice to learn anything, thought Mrs. Gaines. You have to lose something sometimes. And if it was the fish, well, she, Mrs. Gaines, would live without it. Life went on.

◆   ◆   ◆

Anna thought about Jazz's stories of the sea because this felt like the moment of sailing away. He had crossed the ocean in a 40 foot rig; she wondered if she could too. But they could capsize and die. Very young and pregnant, thought Anna; what a heroic way to die. But nothing would ever be completed in her life, if she let the fear grip her. She would die a quitter, worse yet, she would die a loser. She couldn't tolerate losing anything. But competition had nothing to do with this at all. It was not a race.

She didn't have to race Jazz, Jazz with his long legs and his long arms. Anna ran her fingers through the tangles of her red hair, the ends were wet and she put a part of it in her mouth. Then she bit down on it. She looked down at her belly, at what they had made and she imagined she felt something inside there. Jazz was getting out of the tub, dripping water everywhere and this made her mad. She got the urge to hurt him, but she looked down at her reflection in the water, and it was beautiful. There was no need to hurt him at all.

◆　◆　◆

When Mrs. Gaines came to the first stoplight, hunger gripped her, or else all the different signs about food told her she was hungry and she had to eat. She decided the food had to be sweet, so she pulled over at Winchell's, although she and Anna had decided a long time ago that Winchell's was not the best. Splashing a little water as she entered the driveway upset the fish, she imagined.

As she got out of the car she tore the hem of her dress, since it was caught under the seat. This was irritating to her, but not so irritating that she would let it be the main distraction, although she did leave the car without checking on the fish.

Once she was inside she thought it was odd that she couldn't smell the donuts. She pulled a little at the tear on the hem of her dress, examined it, then walked up to the counter and asked for a chocolate old-fashioned. There was only one man sitting in the place, which she felt was odd for a Sunday. She wondered why more people didn't have a sweet tooth, why there weren't more lonely Sunday people in Winchell's.

She looked at the man and he looked back with some interest. She looked at the clock because it occurred to her that the day was passing by her without any knowledge of the time. When the person behind the counter handed her the bag with the donut, she opened it, studying the donut to see that it was the best she could get. She found no reason to ask for the bigger, chocolatier one way in front, which would force the person behind the counter to bend down. It wasn't worth it.

She sat down near the only man and then looked at the person behind the counter. A middle-aged, hard-boned, darker lady, who could be of most any race, Mrs. Gaines decided. She appeared extremely tired, and seemed to be staring at nothing in particular. Mrs. Gaines felt this stare was familiar, and then she realized that this is how Anna looked about the house before she met Jazz.

"I can see you are a respectable lady," the man said.

She looked at him quickly and nodded a vague acknowledgment, then looked at the tear in her dress.

"Your hair is so nicely kept, a root beer brown, but not so neat that it is stuffy. I like that," he said smiling. Mrs. Gaines smiled too, but it wasn't a real smile.

"I mean, I don't mean to be rude, but I think you look quite nice in your raspberry dress, your nice, sensible patent leather shoes, with your curly root beer brown hair." He said this leaning slightly toward her. Mrs. Gaines touched the tear in her dress.

"The grunions will be out tonight, did you know that?" he asked.

Mrs. Gaines shook her head, and then decided she wanted coffee. She sat back down at a table farther away from the man, but this didn't seem to bother him. She looked at him out of the corner of her eye—he wasn't grungy as she'd expected; his hair was a dull color that could have been blond, grey or brown, she couldn't decide—and then she worried a little about vision.

I don't think they allow you to take the grunions out of the ocean anymore," he said. "Against the law now, I believe."

"Really," Mrs. Gaines said, not in the form of a question.

"I mean, you need a permit now over there in Santa Monica."

She looked at him, flaring her nostrils.

"But I love watching those grunions escape the water," he said. "Have you seen the picture, 'Magic Christian'?"

"No, I haven't."

"You know the one with Peter Sellers and Ringo Starr?"

"No, I don't."

"Well, if you did you would remember the last scene where Sellers, who is a millionaire taking care of Ringo Starr, I believe, comes to this pond of shit (if you would excuse my French) whereupon he had posted the sign 'Free Money.' "

"Uh-huh," Mrs. Gaines said, taking a sip of her coffee, and fluttering her lashes as if there was something in her eye.

"And these stuffy English men, you see, come along in their Bowler hats and their canes and their walks, like as if they had a stick up the old ass, (pardon the French) and they come to the pond of shit where Sellers is throwing in big bills and these men scrunch up their noses and stick their canes in like they were fishing to get the bills. But as more of these men came, and the competition gets fierce they get closer and closer, until the greed overcomes them and they're all jumping into the shit and swimming in it to get the big bucks." He was a little red now in the face with excitement.

"Yes, Peter Sellers is always funny," said Mrs. Gaines, trying to think of what she had seen him in.

"Funny how people would risk drowning for anything they thought was free," he said.

"Sounds like a good movie," Mrs. Gaines said.

"People can be the saddest, most misled creatures," said the man, pulling out a cigarette.

He looked very thin to Mrs. Gaines, as he stared beyond the room for a moment.

"So, what do you do?" he asked.

"Nothing. I'm a housewife."

"Well, now, you're not married to your house."

"Of course not. I'm not married at all."

"I see," he said, touching his chin.

"No, you don't see," said Mrs. Gaines, gathering her trash.

"Now, what's the matter, heah? You look like there's a worried nun living inside your head. My grandmother used to look like that all the time."

"I have to be going now," Mrs. Gaines said, standing up now.

"OK, Raspberry. But, hey, listen, if you ever need a divorce from your house, here's my card."

She took it from him, not looking at it until she was outside of the door.

"Bullshit," she said when she saw 'Attorney at Law', and threw the card away with her trash. She felt glad that she had thought of the word "bullshit"; it had been such a very long time.

◆   ◆   ◆

Anna, all alone now in the tub, imagined she was in the boat. She saw the harness and the chain that led to the side of it. She was puzzled at the idea of a harness being in the form of a life jacket. Jazz had explained that it was for any trouble out there in the blue water. Anna had asked why the water was so blue to him, because as she looked down at the water, it was a dull, clear green. Jazz stood there with a towel in his hand, and he explained to her that the blue was what sailors called the deep waters. If you've sailed the blue waters, Jazz said, that meant you've really sailed. When she closed her eyes they were moving, and she could hear Jazz's voice telling her what to do. Then the water got rough and Jazz was yelling although he couldn't have been more than ten inches away. The screaming got unbearable.

"Jazz, let's go back," she yelled.

She imagined that he yelled back, "Anna, marry me."

Anna looked at him squinting so that the elements she imagined, wouldn't get into her eyes. She let only what she thought was the power of his physical presence get to her there, and then she felt sure he loved her. He was so beautiful at that moment, and she thought surely this was something she must have forgotten, how beautiful he could be, and she stared at him before she yelled her answer. He didn't seem to have heard because his expression didn't change. He stared at her with his dark eyes open, not squinting, even though there was all of the water and wind. This was amazing to her. Nothing ever broke him; he didn't even hear what she had said. This made her angry, and now she couldn't even remember what she had said, either.

◆   ◆   ◆

When Mrs. Gaines got in the car, she checked on the fish, who was a little frantic as she slammed the car door. She pulled out of the driveway, and someone honked and flipped her off.

"Everyone has their secret demons," she said aloud to the fish. The person's face had been too angry for a stupid thing like that. There hadn't been any danger there; she didn't do anything to him.

Mrs. Gaines put her seat belt on when she got to the first stoplight. She remembered one of those don't-let-your-friends-drive-drunk commercials, and then she pictured the little fish in back swimming around as a skeleton. This made her laugh, and feel better for the moment. But then the moment was over.

◆   ◆   ◆

Standing in the bathroom, above Anna there in the tub, Jazz thought this is what she wants, for me to worry about her, well then, so be it, I'll marry her.

He needed her. When he stopped looking at Anna, he thought about how responsible he had become. He wished his mother could see him, she wouldn't think he looked like his father now. She wouldn't think he would be just like him. He was going to marry Anna because he loved her, and because that was the least he could do. His mother said that his father always went around making things and then leaving them. So Jazz has to show him the right way. Wherever the fuck he is.

◆ ◆ ◆

Mrs. Gaines was heading down Santa Monica Blvd. trying to remember the easiest way to Anna's street. She could never remember the name of the street either, but she knew there was this funny tree on the corner that stuck out to her, but probably to no one else. Because when she had pointed it out to Anna, she only shrugged. And when Mrs. Gaines looked at it again, really hard, there was nothing peculiar about it at all. It just had these branches that seemed to reach out to you, because they looked like two arms out in front. But she supposed a lot of trees might look that way, especially if you were longing for something you weren't quite sure of.

◆ ◆ ◆

Although Anna was in the tub, she imagined the boat was almost completely on its side, and that she was doing what Jazz yelled at her to do. But she had no idea what was going on exactly. There was fear, but it wasn't gripping—it had more to do with what she might not do right to save the boat, and supposedly, their lives together. When this thought about their lives crossed her mind, she whispered fiercely the Lord's Prayer, the only prayer she knew, and when she got to the line, "forgive us our debts as we forgive our debtors," the water got all over her, so she closed her eyes and gasped as if she had gone under water and come back up after holding her breath for too long. Then she said the line that replaced it—"forgive us our trespasses, as we forgive those who trespass against us." And it seemed like Jazz was far away, because she couldn't hear him, and she couldn't feel him, but they must have been going back because she felt free, like she wasn't still chained to the boat. Maybe she was going to slip into the ocean now, and die there like she'd dreamed she might. Whatever Jazz was yelling to her now was completely incomprehensible. All she remembered seeing before she closed her eyes, was Jazz's terrified face as he was slapping hers.

◆   ◆   ◆

Mrs. Gaines found the tree and turned the corner; as she passed the arms of the tree, she thought it was reaching out for someone else. She imagined the tree was her husband; this is what he did when he was alive. He never wanted anything from her. He always wanted something of someone else. He even called on Anna more. This could be why Anna left her when she did. Because he had left her when he did. But justifications were of a trivial concern to Mrs. Gaines. She found a parking spot close enough to Anna's apartment, but it took her a while to parallel park. She looked at the fish and was amazed at how far its fins reached. Fins like flames.

When Mrs. Gaines got out of the car, she thought a moment and then went back to get the fishbowl. It would make a nice gift for her daughter. Mrs. Gaines smiled at her generous thought, and as she picked up the fishbowl, she whipped the rubber band and plastic baggie off of the top, and blew into the bowl. She watched the ripples and the reaction of the fish.

"I won't decide what you're feeling right now," Mrs. Gaines whispered to the fish. Then she laughed at herself, for talking to it.

◆   ◆   ◆

Anna wasn't responding, so Jazz was panicking, and slapping her too many times, he realized, for it to do any good. She was out, and they shouldn't play these games, he thought.

"Anna, wake up!" Jazz yelled in her ear. He splashed water on her face. She didn't move and he saw that he was doing the wrong thing. As he propped her up, lifted her out and laid her down, he imagined that what he was supposed to do was hold her nose and breathe into her mouth.

"We shouldn't play these games anymore, Anna," he said in between breaths. She started to cough a little, and then some of the water came up and out of her mouth. Jazz held her and swayed her in his arms. She cried a little, and after a long while, she started humming to herself. He took her body up closer to his and started kissing her bruised skin. And as he went on kissing her, he felt his own bruises. She had opened her eyes and was looking above as if she saw something. Something that couldn't really have been there. This was endearing to Jazz and his kiss became passionate, and she sighed.

◆　◆　◆

Mrs. Gaines knocked on the door with her right fist, her left arm encircling the fishbowl. She waited there, no answer. She knocked louder and when still there was no answer she tried the door which wasn't locked at the bottom, but bolted at the top. And then she remembered she had a key from the time Jazz left his at her place one afternoon. He had come over to say he was worried about Anna and she had told him the best thing to do was to leave her. Well, he didn't leave her, although he had left his key, and Mrs. Gaines was able to make a copy and return it to him the next day. When she got there he was carving a little figure out of wood. He wouldn't tell her what the figure was; he told her she'd have to wait until it was finished before she could find out. Then Mrs. Gaines told herself she didn't really care what it was. She gave him the key and left, and the following three days she called at different hours, waiting for them not to answer. Every time she called, Jazz answered and she would hang up each time, except for once when it was Anna. Mrs. Gaines hesitated. Her daughter had a sweet voice. But then Mrs. Gaines hung up on her too, and it hurt just a little. He was always there, and she never got to see what that figure was. She didn't care though. All these things Mrs. Gaines thought about as she looked for the key.

♦ ♦ ♦

Anna's arms were stretched out above her head and every time Jazz thrusted as hard as he could, she felt it reached way inside of her belly, like he was trying to break her, like he was trying to free something there. She felt all of her spine being mashed into the floor, the floor burning her bone, his body wet with sweat and bathwater, heavy on top of her, and she grabbed his back and sunk her nails in. She opened her eyes, looked at Jazz, something in him she didn't recognize, but she felt it was sincere. And she looked up at the ceiling, something up there was free that he couldn't have, and it was flying above them. And it made her feel at once old and ageless to know she could call it down from there any time she wanted. Any moment now, she would.

♦ ♦ ♦

Once Mrs. Gaines was inside she heard the water running, and still carrying the fishbowl she rushed to the bathroom splashing everywhere as she went. She got to the bedroom door. She heard noises, noises she hadn't heard since her husband died. Her stomach tightened, her tongue numbed, she couldn't swallow, her throat was dry. The knot was lowering now and she was choking, but she kept going to take what it was she must see. The water was running in the tub and spilling out on the floor, flooding the room; her daughter was making those noises, and she was heaving, lying under that man. Mrs. Gaines dropped the fishbowl, glass, water flying, splattering, splintering everywhere, Mrs. Gaines running faster, out of the room, out of that house, faster than she'd ever run before. And Anna just lay there, her thighs squeezing Jazz's hips, while the fish flipped around on the floor, free, its fins flaming, its gills pumping.

Meeting for Breakfast

Wednesday morning, Jana and Ferdinand enter Hugo's. They are seated in the back corner, too close to the wall. Ferdinand snaps open the menu; Jana situates her springy skirt so huge it encases the chair. Ferdinand is small, brown with a solid build, and a face calling question of origin—India, Hawaii, Thailand, the Philippines. Jana is tall, dark as smoke, with a large crooked smile; ten, long, fat braids give her a Jamaican, West Indian, British black look. Jana glances around the room. Two men stare from two tables over.

"What are you having, Sweety?" with his pampering voice, Ferdinand wins back her attention.

"A spinach omelet," she says.

"I think I want pasta," he says, looking it over again.

"Pasta, so early?" She smiles at him lovingly, then sits up

straight in her chair.

"Why not?" he grins, snaps the menu shut.

"Did I tell you I went out with Trevor and his friend the other day, just walking around Santa Monica? Anyway, when we were leaving the restaurant this old white drunk on the street, says to us, 'How're you *niggers* doing this evening?' "

Ferdinand shakes his head, squeezes her hand which brushes softly back and forth across the table.

"It was my first time, you know, being called that. All of us were quiet until I pointed out the sunset. And we breathed in relief. But even as we drove home, the music loud, I could feel our anger, depression still hanging so heavy in the air."

Ferdinand nods, playing now tenderly with her fingers. Jana looks at him, a smile breaking through. The waitress approaches the table, announces there is no orange juice, and leaves to get them coffee before they can order.

"I only have until 12:30 today, I have to go into work a little early," he says.

"That's OK," she says, fiddling with her spoon. "How's Connie?"

"She's all right. Lonely, you know. We have to find her a boyfriend."

"What happened to the man she was seeing?"

"Well, I told you he's married, and that's been going on for years. I bet she would love Trevor, though, don't you think?"

"I don't think he'd like her."

"Connie loves black men in their early 40s," he says.

Jana moves her hands together in a tight tunnel through the air, toward Ferdinand and back.

"One physical type—so *fucked* up," she says.

The waitress brings the coffee, then leaves again before

they can order. Ferdinand sighs.

"I know. But she says she likes the way they make her feel in bed. No nonsense."

"Uh-huh. Like they're all the same. Fucked up. Anyway, Trevor is too young by her standards. Thank God."

Ferdinand laughs, then tries to get a waiter's eye.

"Excuse me, but we haven't ordered yet," he says to the waitress who holds up a one-minute finger. "And we're *hungry,*" he says to Jana, putting the menu down again.

"You know Connie grew up in a very white environment. She never had to deal with anyone of color until college, and I think she is simply naive about other kinds of people that she doesn't understand."

"Yeah, so. Does that excuse it?"

"No. I know. Fetish. And when I tell her how much it offends me to hear jokes about Chinese people, about black people, she doesn't understand. She thinks it's harmless, like I'm being too sensitive," he says.

Jana nods, sips her coffee.

"Really, she is racist, and I think in her next life she will be born a person of color, and have to deal with it," he says with force in his voice.

A waiter finally walks up, Ferdinand gives him the exasperated look. They order, Ferdinand specifying exactly how he wants his pasta, and a good bottle of water. When Jana refuses a cup of fruit, Ferdinand orders it anyway, never missing a chance to indulge her.

"You're into reincarnation now, Ferdi?"

"Well, I don't know. 'It could happen,'" he says in a mock voice.

◆ ◆ ◆

Jana wakes up, breathing fast, holding onto the sheet beneath her with both hands wound tightly in fists. She looks at the clock, 6:30 AM. Her head falls back slowly on the pillow. She lets go of the sheet, rolls over onto her stomach. She has had violent dreams before—knives, guns, blood gushing—but never this real, never this intense. Jana turns back around in bed, sits up, head spinning. On her small table next to the bed are her birth control pills. She picks them up, turns the case around in her hand, lies back, closes her eyes. She can see a bit of the dream again as she squeezes her eyes shut, trying at once to forget, and to call it back. She sees Connie's loft, she sees her hands around Connie's throat, and she can almost feel the skin getting under her fingernails. Jana opens her eyes, gets up. Cold, she puts on a T-shirt, punches the Thursday pill out of its slot, swallows it, then throws the case back to the bed. She goes into the bathroom, washes her face; when she looks in the mirror, she finds the reflection ugly. Sitting on the toilet as the early morning piss gushes, she wonders if she could wake Ferdinand in an hour. She decides against it because she doesn't want to scare him. Then again, maybe it wouldn't scare him at all. She gets up, goes to the desk for her typewriter. She figures if she could just type the dream out in a letter to Trevor, the sound of the keys would make her feel a lot better. Jana decides she'll call Trevor as soon as it is a decent hour, to see if they can have lunch today. She doesn't want to be alone—not the whole day—but working at home really gives her little choice. Her fingers fly over the keys, she lets her trust in him overwhelm her. When she gets to the part where she has to type, "Connie was dead, I actually killed her," she looks in fright at the paper, as if it proved her guilt. She puts the word "dream" many more times in the letter, as she works her way down. Trevor will understand, she says to herself.

◆　◆　◆

It has been three days since breakfast with Ferdinand. So as the phone rings first thing in the morning, Jana says, Ferdi, out loud as she picks it up. Ferdinand's voice comes in short gasps, unclear. Jana tells him she can't hear him, and she knows he is in tears. She hears him suck in his breath, exhale, and she can tell now he is dragging on a cigarette. She waits for him to pull himself together, but she is scared.

"Jana, Connie is dead," he gets out in a fast snatch of air.

"What?!"

"She was *killed*. Three nights ago—I just found out."

"*What?* No, God, Ferdi, I can't . . . "

"Remember I told you she was going to have a film crew at her place? They were going to use her loft window to shoot a scene of Loni Anderson being pushed to her death? Remember?" he asks, his words coming faster.

"And how we laughed! But . . . "

"Well something happened, I don't know, that made her leave the loft, made her go into the alley next to the building, my God! There were police there, as usual with the film crews, and those *dicks,* those fucking *assholes,* let her get strangled in the alley . . . "

"*What?* What are you saying? *Who* could . . . "

"A mugger, a street person, a thug, I don't know, I mean . . . " Ferdinand exhales, and she hears his breathing go fast again. Then something comes out like a screeching gasp; Jana squeezes the receiver, tries to be calm.

"Ferdi, listen to me. I'm coming over. I'll be there in 20 minutes. Can you hang on, Ferd?" she asks, her hand over her chest.

"Yeah, just . . . please . . . " he says. Dead air.

Jana looks at the phone as if it were the killer. She runs to the bathroom mirror, puts lipstick on. She wants to be pretty for Ferdinand, she wants to be strong. She throws on a sweater, grabs a scarf, slides her feet into espadrilles. Nothing of sense is going through her head, and when she looks at the clock, she can't read it.

Getting in the car, the squeak of the door like a chalkboard scratch shoots under her skin. She drives, trying to hum with the radio, then she rushes station changes. She stops on a classical, bass viol moans. She cries, wiping her eyes at stoplights. In the mirror she is disgusted by her vanity. A guy stops next to her in a beat-up blue Karmann Ghia; he gives her a loving stranger's smile. She looks at him gratefully, turns the corner for Ferdinand's as the light turns red.

The door is open; she walks in. Ferdinand smokes on the couch, next to him is the cat with a leg in a red cast. Ferdinand puts the cigarette out. The ashtray overflows; he opens his arms to let her in. Ferdinand buries his face in her chest, and as she holds him she feels him shake. When his tears wet her sweater through, she rocks him. It is a great while before she can feel him calm. That's when she lifts his face to look at him, kisses his cheeks, holds his head up.

"Let me get you something to drink, some water or something," she whispers.

Jana goes into the kitchen, brings down two glasses, then a third when she spots the Sake. She brings in the two glasses of water, then on the second trip, the Sake, and the one glass. Ferdinand is drinking the water, but as soon as she sets down the Sake-filled glass, he picks it up, gulps it down. Jana puts the bottle to her mouth.

"What time is it?" Ferdinand asks.

"I don't know," she looks around. "Where is the clock, Ferdi?"

He points down the hall, Jana gets up to go to his bedroom. She already feels the Sake working when she sits down on the bed to see the clock.

"It's 9:30 Ferd!" she calls from the room, still sitting on the bed, her head spinning. The dream plays again in her head; she tries to squeeze it out with her hands, but instead feels Connie's skin under her fingernails.

"God, stop it!" Jana yells out loud.

Ferdi comes in with his water, looks at Jana on his bed. He sits next to her, puts his arm around her, kisses her where the sweater has slipped off her shoulder.

"You're not going to work today," Jana says.

"No, it's Saturday," he says. "The funeral is tomorrow."

"Do you want me to go with you?" she asks, hoping he doesn't.

"You don't have to, Sweety."

"Well, no. But if you need me . . . "

"It's OK, really. Elvie is flying in tonight. He and I will go together. Don't worry about it."

Ferdinand lays his head in her lap, closes his eyes. She strokes his thick black hair. Fear builds up so loud it is deafening. When he is heavy with sleep, she slips out from under him, covers his body with the messy sheets. She goes to the living room, walks a circle around it, stops in front of the cat with his broken leg, he opens one eye to stare back at her.

"Tell Ferdi I'll be back in an hour," she tells the cat. "I just need to see someone. I'll be right back."

She never realized how close Trevor's place is to Ferdinand's. As she goes up the steps, panic sets in. She bangs on the door several times before she hears anything. When the waiting gets unbearable, she starts pushing on the door. Trevor opens it, and she flumps in. Trevor is in a T-shirt and jeans with the buttons undone; he wipes the sleep from his eyes when she falls into his arms.

"What is it? Jan, what is it?" he asks softly, holding her up. He kicks the door closed, moves her with him farther into the room.

"Hold me."

He rubs her back, one thick braid slips in between his fingers. He holds onto it tightly, his other arm strong around her waist. He puts both hands on her face so he can see her.

"Tell me, Jana, what happened?"

Sniffling, she wipes her eyes with the back of her hand, looks at his forehead, tense with worry. She runs her fingers across the line there, down to the few stray hairs between his eyebrows, back up to where the tiny curls begin on his head.

"Hey, hey, *hey*, Jana, *talk* to me. What is it?" he whispers, holding her still.

Jana concentrates on his face, puts her finger on his nose,

then down to the space where it sinks in just above his lips, now slides it gently down so he can give her fingertip a soft wet kiss. He holds on to her, her mouth open, kissing his neck, slowly, then his ear. She pulls back away far enough to see his face again.

"You are the color of dark honey," she whispers to him, and he smiles. She takes his hand from her waist, and slowly again, puts each finger to her mouth. As their breathing comes heavier, she pulls on his finger with her mouth, sucking it so it hurts. As if worrying for a moment that this is wrong for a first time, Trevor pulls away from her an inch, a short hesitation, then he roughly brings her face to his lips. They fall to the floor.

Later, they lie there for a long time, still, silent. Jana's thigh sticky between his, they are gone now into a half-sleep.

When she feels him stir beneath her, she wakes him up.

"Trevor," she begins tentatively. "I killed her."

"What? *What* are you talking about?" he opens his eyes.

"I killed her," she says with definition. Trevor moves out abruptly from under her.

"Jana, *what* are you talking about?"

"Didn't you get my letter?"

"*Which* letter?" he asks, irritated.

"The one about the dream, Trevor. Connie's dead. It wasn't a *dream.* I killed her."

Trevor sits up, holds onto his head, looks at the floor, looks at their legs, their feet still entangled. He snatches himself from her, stares her straight in the eye. She puts her arms around her breasts to cover them. He sits there for a long time, moves his hand awkwardly back across his spine. He straightens up, his eyes widening.

"It couldn't have been a dream," she continues. "I can't remember driving down there, but I can feel the skin under my fingernails! I must have killed her, because she *is dead.*"

Trevor looks at her in horror then around the room. Jana feels it ticking, about to go off. She reaches for her clothes; he grabs her arm, squeezes it firmly.

"Now, you listen to me. You are confused," he says with anger. "You are going to have to *slow down.* There is no way you killed her, just because you found out she was dead. You *dreamed* you were strangling her—a very *strange* coincidence—but, the thing is, you must be psychic."

"No. I don't remember going downtown but I can

feel the skin under my fingernails. You see? That couldn't have been a dream. She was *strangled,* Trevor! Ferdinand called me this morning! I am so fucking *scared!* I don't know what to do. What should I do?" she asks, getting hysterical.

"Now stop it!" he says, more angrily now. "Get a hold of yourself!" On his knees now, he shakes her up. "Why would you kill her? For what reason? This is insane! You went to sleep, you had a dream, it is as simple as that. When did you wake up? You were home! Nothing was different, it was only a dream!

"Dreams are only . . . the . . . the . . . subconscious trying to resolve the day's events. If you really killed her, you would have been dreaming about what you were going to do now that you have done it, rather than dreaming that you were doing it—understand me? Yes?" he says, still holding onto her shoulders.

Jana nods, tears begin, and she shakes her head.

"Now of course, I am right," he says softer now, "There is no way you did it. You were just working off frustration, what you were feeling, like you said in the letter. Your resentment came out in the dream. Or you are psychic. Right?"

"You have to tear up that letter, Trevor."

"Of course, *yes,*" he says, beginning to sound hysterical himself, "I'm going to tear it up now. But you have to try and forget all of this. Put the whole damn mess behind you!"

Trevor stands, grabs his clothes with him, disappears into the bedroom. Jana sits on the floor, still naked, hugging herself. She hears Trevor rustling around in there as she puts her clothes on. When she hears him close the bathroom door, she walks out of his place and into the street, deciding the thing to do is go home.

◆　◆　◆

Wednesday morning again, Jana and Ferdinand meet for breakfast at Hugo's. This time they are seated in front by the window. Jana's fat braids are gathered up together on top of her head in a big ponytail with a giant red ribbon. She smoothes her skirt out from under her, wiggling in her chair like a flirt. Ferdinand watches her, smiles; they look at each other like they have gotten over everything. Then Jana feels a twinge of panic and suspicion at this quick recovery in Ferdinand.

"What are you having, Sweety?" he asks.

"An omelet, of course," she says, smiling. Jana looks around her, wiggles in her chair again, then scoots into the table to get closer to Ferdinand.

"How was the funeral? Or shouldn't I be asking?"

"I really don't remember it," he says, looking at the menu. "Should we get french toast too?"

"Oh. You don't want to talk about it."

"It's not that at all. It's just that I made my peace with it."

"Yeah? Well, that's good, Ferd, I'm glad. I really didn't know her well, but it's been hard seeing you go through this. I worry about you."

"Well, I made my peace with it. I said to myself, Connie will come back as a better person."

"You really believe that, Ferd? I didn't know you were so into it."

"Yeah? Well, it's nothing to 'get into,' you just know that it makes sense. And Connie really was a racist. She is better off dead."

"*What?*"

"You heard me. She's better off dead. Now she can come back and deal with things as a person of color."

"But Ferdi, you sound insane. And you can't be sure of something like that."

"Don't be silly, Sweety," he says with an edge in his voice.

The waiter comes for their order, Ferdinand does all of the talking, specifying exactly how he wants it, how Jana wants it.

"Ferd, that's really a little too much food, don't you think?"

"We'll eat it."

Ferdinand shifts in his seat, then they are both fidgeting. Jana looks around the room, back at him. She puts her hand out on the table, her fingers do a drum roll. Ferdinand laughs, puts his hand over hers, squeezes.

"Ferdi?"

"Yeah?"

"You mind telling me something else . . . about Connie?"

"What?"

"How did you find out, I mean, that she was dead?"

"I saw it on Entertainment Tonight."

"You're kidding me, aren't you?" she says, beginning to laugh in spite of her own fright.

"It's because of the film crew, you know, it was a big scandal for them. The owner of the location they're shooting in is strangled in the alley while they're in her place, while these people are all over the street? You know. Vans up and down the block? The director was such a dick. I could tell by his attitude that . . . "

"You mean on TV?"

"Yes, on TV. He just had *attitude,* like why are you tripping on *us.* He said, 'This is downtown, and we all know it is not one of the safest areas in LA.' He said it with *so much* attitude. You know, like, Leave us alone, and go bother the homeless who probably did it."

The waiter brings their coffee, juice, and rolls. Jana butters a roll as Ferdinand watches.

"I have this twitch in my lip, that's driving me crazy—can you see it?" he asks.

Jana leans over the table, watches his lips as he sits perfectly still. Finally they twitch.

"Yeah, I see it. It'll go away," she says, biting into the roll.

Ferdinand sips his coffee, swallows hard.

"So where did you go that day when you left me sleeping?" he asks.

"To Trevor's."

"Why?"

"I don't know. I needed to. We're beginning to get close."

"What do you mean 'beginning to get close'? It seems as though you have already had your drama together. Don't you think it's time to give it a rest?"

"I don't know what you mean. With me there are always battles, we went a little fast, had to slow down. But he's a good person. He's a good friend."

"I know what it's like with you. Maybe you trust him too much."

"What is that supposed to mean?"

"Maybe you don't know him well enough, yet, to trust him with everything. To just go running to him with your trouble. How long has it been?"

"A while. I've known him long enough to know I *like* him. And trust him."

Ferdinand shrugs, the waiter brings their food. He puts his fork in, pushes the egg around.

"So what happened with Trevor, when you ran to him that day?"

"We slept together."

"You did not."

"Yeah, we did," she says, smiling.

"You little slut."

"Ferdinand!"

"Just kidding," he says, twisting his fork in the food. "So, are you 'in love' now?"

"I can't be sure. No. You can't tell things like that until you're sure. But it was nice. It's been a while for me, and he made me feel good."

"Yeah? Well, that's great," he says, still twisting his fork.

"Lighten up. You are so protective, Ferdinand, it's absurd.

Trevor wouldn't play with my mind."

"Was he *good?*"

"Ferdi," she says, slapping his hand with the fork in it, "Drop it. I don't like your tone."

"Are you seeing him tonight?"

"Did you hear me? Let's drop it. You're scaring me. Okay? This is *not* you. Please stop."

Sitting up straight in her chair, Jana looks Ferdinand in the eye. He is staring at her now as if he doesn't know her.

"Come on now," she says, softening. "You haven't eaten a thing."

"I don't have much time. I should be getting to work early. Let me call and see how much time I have."

She watches him leave the table.

Jana's head spins again after gulping her coffee down. She wants to tell Ferdinand about the dream to clear her conscience with him, but not now with this mood. She was feeling these past few days that Trevor was right, that she hadn't done it. But now with Ferdinand's weird vibes, she can't be sure of anything.

Ferdinand comes back to the table, gathers his things, kisses her on the cheek.

"Honey, I am leaving you two twenties to cover it. I have to go, I'm sorry," he says, bending down to kiss her again, this time on the mouth, and with force.

"Before you go, Ferdi, tell me . . . "

"What?"

"Was I the first person you called when you found out?"

"Yes. I called you first thing."

"Okay," she says, squeezing his hand. "That's good to know." Ferdinand smiles, walks out of the room.

◆   ◆   ◆

Jana opens the door, Trevor is standing there. His brows meet with tension. She lets him in, keeping her heart in place. He pushes the sleeves of his sweater up his arms. Jana wipes the paint from her hands onto her messy shirt, backs away from him. His big eyes fill, as if waiting for her to speak first.

"I called you the other night. Did you get the message?" she asks dryly.

"No. But I'm here now, if that's all right."

"You want something to drink?"

"No, I can't stay. I came to see how you're doing."

"I'm OK, I think. I just keep going back and forth."

Trevor sits down on the couch. Soon she sits next to him, so close she can feel his breathing. She hopes he cannot hear her heart thumping.

"Nice blue trim."

"Thanks."

"Need help with it?"

"No thanks."

"Well," he sighs. "I want to talk about the other day."

"Yeah?"

"First of all, it was a weird morning. In tears you come to my place . . . then . . . we make love for the first time, *then* . . . you're telling me you killed someone, then, when I walk out of the room for a second, you're *gone.*"

"Yeah," she says, not looking at him.

"And, it all is still a little too much for me to . . . to . . . put

in order, and I want to say now, that, we should try and . . .
calm it down."

"Yeah . . . "

"You mean a lot to me, and I want to . . . give us time, give
it a chance," he looks down at his lap, then up at her.

"So . . . " she says, leaning away from him.

"Yeah, 'so,' I came to say that, basically, and to see how
you're doing."

"Okay." She slowly turns her head from him, then
straightens up in defiance. "Well, I don't need . . . " The
telephone ring cuts her off. "Should I pick up?"

"I don't care," he shrugs.

"Hello?" she holds on tighter to the phone. "Ferdinand?
Where are you?"

"I'm home, can I come by?"

"Sure. Well, you know, Trevor's here," she says, grabbing
Trevor's wrist as he gets up. "Where are you going," she
mouths to him. He points to the kitchen, pulls away from
her.

"I'm sorry, did I *interrupt* something?" Ferdinand asks.

"I wouldn't have picked up if you did."

"Well, this can wait."

"What is it, Ferdi?"

"It can wait. Call me when your lover is gone." He hangs
up.

"What's the matter?" Trevor asks, coming out of the
kitchen with two glasses of water. He hands one to her, she
holds it staring out into space.

"Ferdinand is *tripping.*"

"One of his closest friends was killed."

"Yes, but . . . "

"But, what?" he shifts his weight.

"I was thinking about everything he's said to me. It sounds weird."

"Like?"

"He called me first thing after he heard. It was Saturday morning when he called me, but he told me he found out from watching Entertainment Tonight."

"So?"

"So, it's on in the evening which means he waited hours and hours, all night before he called."

"Well, seems to me he couldn't be sure of anything at a time like that."

"But I know him. If he said he called me first thing, he called me first thing."

"He couldn't have called you first thing if he found out at night. Anyway, it would take a while for it to sink in if you found out on TV that your friend was killed! Look, all we have to do is find out *when* she died. So how can we do that?"

"Call the coroner's office? . . . No, they'd never give up information to just anyone," she says, holding onto her head. "I know. I'll call Elvie!"

"Okay, call 'Elvie,' whoever the hell that is," Trevor says, walking away to the bathroom.

Jana is about to talk to the machine when Elvie picks up. They go through sweet greetings then Jana takes a serious tone.

"Sorry to bother you, but Ferdi has been under such a tremendous strain—as I'm sure you have been—but I need to ask you a question."

"What strain?"

"When was Connie killed?"

"You're kidding me, right?"

"No. I need to know when?"

"Did Ferdinand put you up to this? Tell him this isn't funny."

"He told me you flew in for the funeral, so I just assumed . . ."

"What the hell is going on?"

"You mean you don't know? I have to go, El. Let me get back to you." Jana hangs up, Trevor is watching.

"Is she dead, or not?!" Jana yells, paces. "What the fuck is going on?!"

"Calm down. We'll figure this bullshit out," he says, holding her.

"Will you go with me downtown?" she asks.

"Of course."

"Yes. Okay, we'll do that," she says, goes into the bedroom for a jacket.

"But what will going down there solve?" he calls to her.

"If she is dead, for one thing," she says, coming back, pulling the jacket over her head. "Ferdinand is obviously out of his mind."

◆ ◆ ◆

Trevor and Jana wait in The Pantry for hours. It's 6 AM, Sunday morning. Trevor squeezes a napkin, dips it into the cold stale coffee at the bottom of his cup. Jana, wired, slides back and forth across the booth seat until he grabs her arm.

"Let's go home, already. This is too much."

"Just ten more minutes. I'll try his house again," she says, pleading with her eyes.

"This is absurd. We should go get some sleep, make calls later, straighten everything out." He waits, and she is not looking at him. "Let's fucking go home!" he says, shoving a plate with half a muffin across the table so that it bounces off the wall.

"Please, Trevor, *ten* more minutes. Please. For me."

"For you? Just do this for you? I go running across town with you in search of someone who is dead, who *may* not be dead, we find nothing—of course, and what the hell *could* we find at the door of her building—we can't get in, then you call Ferdinand, tell him to meet you, and we wait here for this fucking jerk for hours. And I *hate* cafeterias! What the hell is the point?"

Jana yanks her arm back from him.

"At least I know I didn't do it. I was never there."

"Of course you didn't do it! *I fucking told you that!*"

"Okay, then leave me here, go on! I don't care," she says, squinting her eyes at him.

"What-ev," he says, getting up, "I don't need this shit."

She watches him cross the room, hitting the backs of empty chairs. He turns at the door, looks at Jana like he hates her, but her expression stops him. They look at each other; Trevor breaks into a loving smile. Then Ferdinand walks through the door, Trevor watches him as he passes, heading for Jana. Jana gets up, leads Ferdinand back to the door to catch Trevor who has turned and walked out.

"Where the *hell* have you been?" she asks him, still pulling him along. He doesn't resist. "Trevor, wait a minute!" she calls to him, he stops.

Ferdinand pulls away, straightening his jacket, his body puffed up like an iguana. Exhausted, Trevor begins to laugh uncontrollably. Ferdinand gets redder in the face.

"Trevor, stop it already," she says, looking at him then back at Ferdinand. "Ferdi, I talked to Elvie, he never came here, he didn't even *know!* Ferdi, what is going on?"

"Okay, so I was wrong. She's *not* dead."

"*What?* Where are you going?" she says, following him as he heads for his car around the corner. Many paces behind is Trevor, still laughing. Ferdinand opens the car door, pulls a crowbar out from under the suitcases.

Trevor doesn't hear him when he says to Jana, "No one laughs at me," so when he sees her go down, and he's running to them, Ferdinand has already hit her twice with it. And when Trevor grabs the crowbar from him, after he's pushed him, thinking he had knocked him out, he gets on his knees, bends over her, his head on her chest, his ear to her breast, her stomach, his hand feeling everywhere on her body for a breath, any movement at all. When he finds her pulse, Trevor darts up, with her blood on him, he runs for the phone, screaming for help. Ferdinand, who has managed to get in his car, gasses the engine, and drives off.

Paris

Sunnie's Forehead

I find the glass eye on the deck of the boat mid-September, then I meet Berger in the metro two days after that, 1 AM, waiting on the last train. One eye follows me, the other one doesn't. Tiny puff of hair beneath his bottom lip, Auschwitz buzzcut, boxy brown suit. I hold onto my camera bag, but he looks too expensive to roll me. He leans against the post, lights a cigarette, waves the pack at me. Doesn't look gay, nor the type who collects black men. I turn my back.

A chick descends the stair, slows, seeing two guys in the otherwise empty station, still she has that French cool. Wrinkled dress, brown messy hair, no make-up, curled slim lip, confident of a beauty she doesn't truly have.

She bums a cigarette, asks him the time. I hear his German accent. The train squeals, we enter, one, two, three, equally spaced apart. The orange seats, our faces reflective, trying to hide mutual curiosity. Perfect photograph.

I finger the eye in my pocket. Berger—whose name I don't know yet of course—gets antsy. Is my eye connected to his? The psychic thing I go in and out of, depending on how long I can stand it.

I let go of the eye, grasp the camera bag in my lap. He turns away. I put my hand in my pocket again, squeeze it, roll it like a marble. He shuts his eyes as if pained. Power, terror grips me, like the first time you hold a pistol, aim, fire.

The chick gets off at the third stop. She lingers at the door as it opens, probably thinking one of us will follow her. One of his eyes is on her, the other on the rail under her. I touch the eye in my pocket, he smiles the Mona Lisa, and I note his charm. I'm not into men, don't understand it, nor judge it. Berger is handsome, in that 40ish handsome, East German intellectual kind of way.

I get off, so does he. Some anxiety again, annoyance, maybe excitement.

"Excusez-moi . . . "

"Oui . . . "

"Ah, American. Excuse me, please, I just wondered if . . . "

"Look, I'm not interested."

"I just wondered, if you please, have a moment?"

One of his eyes pleads, the other doesn't care.

"Well?"

"I'm, how-do-you-say? I need . . . well, do you have a moment, please, for a drink?"

"No, I don't. If you'd excuse me."

As I turn my back, he lays his hand on my shoulder. My

stomach flutters, I stop.

"What's happening, man? What do you need?"

"I need to talk, yes? If it's okay. One drink, if you please."

I want to take the eye from my pocket, throw it down the street.

"I'm kind of in a hurry, man."

"One drink. Or I could walk you to your hotel."

"Okay. One drink."

I don't want him to know where I'm staying, which is not a hotel. This woman's letting me house sit. I don't think she'd appreciate him knowing where she lives; she is so well-known, her image all over the place.

We walk together in the dark cobbled street. He's quiet, smoking.

"Uh, it 'tis how-you-say, 'one of those nights,' you understand."

I nod, see the stones glitter under the streetlamp.

"You live here?" I ask him.

"No. Ah, yes, here it 'tis."

He welcomes me to the door with his arm, one eye is on the bar's entrance, the other on the window. The light spots his hair so it appears as cut crystals. The angle of his nose makes the bone seem to wander with his eye and his fleshy, uneven upper lip. Perfect photograph.

"Bourbon, please, and what would you like?"

"Mineral water."

Berger holds onto his drink, presses his lips with the glass a bit too long before sipping. We exchange names, the bartender wipes the counter, Berger turns to look at me, I drink, remember we hadn't clinked glasses, and I suddenly regret this.

"I don't mean to be . . . what 'tis the word . . . weighted."

"Heavy?"

"Yes, yes. This past year, it 'tas been . . . hard."

I'm annoyed at the heavy pauses, wishing I knew some German.

"My brother died last year," he continues.

"I'm sorry." I move the camera bag from between us.

"He was only 41. My mother was . . . " he clears his throat, "she and I . . . we never got . . . "

"Along . . ."

"Yes, never get on . . . But this changes, yes? Everything it changes when you have such a . . . "

"Loss . . ."

"This sadness, yes. Then my sister . . . well, I don't mean . . ."

"Go on."

"Not to burden you, yes. But my sister, well, she is ill . . . how you say?"

"Sick . . ."

"Yes, she is ter-minal . . . "

"*Ill* . . . I'm sorry."

"Yes. And she has a child, you know. I *love* this child."

"Are you the oldest?"

"No no. I'm the baby, yes. My sister, she is 45 last Tuesday, my brother is, was, 41," He puts his palms together, sighs, then places them on the bar. "My mother, you know, she is . . . adopted, all of her brothers and sisters adopted, and this makes . . . "

"Her distant?"

"She never felt really, very close to any of us. My sister is a kind of mother to me, yes?"

"How old are you?"

"Thirty-nine. And you?"

"Twenty-eight."

"Yes. I have friends twenty-eight years old."

"Really?"

"Well, yes. Many friends, many ages, but I have a lot of young . . . well, I'm a writer."

"You meet a lot of young people?"

"In my country a lot of young people know my writing."

"I see."

"But you see, yes, I don't have many friends. I mean, I never really *talk* like this."

With both hands he feels his breast pockets, hits them, then the back of his pants. Extracts a wallet.

"Please, look at this."

He hands me a photograph, blurred and bubbled around the image. Artfully done. Too artfully.

"It 'twas in a fire, yes. In a photo album, the page, the . . . how you say?"

"Plastic . . . "

"The plastic preserved it, but when the photo was pulled from the plastic, this is how it happens."

A girl, taken in the late sixties probably, white dress, beautiful legs, pained expression.

"Look closer, yes. You recognize?"

"Wait a minute . . . " I am so stunned, I could hit him. "How did you know?! Have you been following me?"

One eye tries calming me down, the other gives up.

"No. Lidya described me to . . . "

"Me to you?"

"Yes. We have been friends many years, Lidya and I."

"How do I know you're not just some crazy fuck trying to get to her?"

"Excuse me. Please. Do not leave. What 'tis it you say?"

"I'm outta here."

I am through the door as he grabs my arm, I pull away, keep walking.

"If you follow me, I'll kick your ass, man. You hear?"

"Please, my friend, you are angry. You must listen, *please.* I am true. I do not have to show you this photograph. I want you to know my . . . history."

"What do you want with Lidya? An *interview?*"

"Of course not!" he flicks his hand sharply near his brow. "When you talk to her, you will be sorry you act in this manner."

"Out of my way, man."

I continue down the street, not looking back. I can feel he is not lying but I don't want to be involved. Lidya has so many "histories" and she gets caught up in the telling, caught up in the watching me experience them, until I am drained. Empty.

I reach the building, the doorman opens up, I squeeze the eye in my pocket. I want to throw it away. But then I would be throwing away the feeling I had on the deck of the boat, the sun beating down, the glare that hit me when I discovered it. There was a presence I felt on that boat, an almost fatherly presence. There was a memory I could not get to, a recognition. Then there was a terror too.

I look out the window. Berger is not there. Still I feel as if he is watching. I have no way of reaching Lidya, but I don't care to tell her. Episodes happen.

When you dream of someone who doesn't know you,

someone who's never seen you before, you take something from them. Perhaps they stir wherever they are, feel some small part taken. You see this when you look at Lidya. All of the missing small bits.

I remain intact, never taking from myself. I remain intact, never searching for my pieces.

Everywhere in the room, photographs of Lidya. The city glows through the window. Her image everywhere, catching the light. I try pushing Berger out of my mind, try clearing my head to concentrate on the usual. I brush the satin trim of the sheet against my lips, my chin, my neck. I turn over, turn over again. Press against the mattress. Finally, I jerk off. Afterwards, I feel guilty. Usually, never. I get up.

Everywhere, photographs of Lidya. In her bedroom, in the corridor, in the living room. Accompanying her, in a few, are the men in her life. Framed magazine covers, page 6 parties. I could go back to New York. I've found little work here. If I could afford it, I'd move to a hotel. If I had courage, I'd really look into it. Myself.

It occurs to me that Berger's intentions may have little to do with her. I think he only wanted to make me feel comfortable, familiar. He's the kind of guy who doesn't have a clue about how to put someone at ease.

I set up the tripod, the lights, stand with my back to the camera, facing the blinds. I squeeze. I turn my profile to the camera, watch my shadow, squeeze.

In the morning, I receive a message from Lidya. She says she hopes I am having a good time, and wonders if there's anything I need, or anything I want to tell her. I panic, which is ridiculous, because surely she is only being polite. But what if Berger contacted her? What if Berger were some kind of trustworthiness test? Then, had I failed?

She left her cell phone number, which she hadn't given me before, still I leave word with her assistant that everything is fine, Thank you.

A week later I see Berger near the Luxembourg. It's the one day I do not carry the eye in my pocket. I approach him, apologize for the night in the bar. We walk.

"My sister lives here. So close to this beautiful garden. She has a nurse. The child is yet in Austria . . . with our mother."

"How do you . . . "

"I must take you to see her, yes?"

"I don't really have time, I . . . "

"I would like if you would go with me to visit her. *Please,* my friend."

"Okay. Sure. Whatever."

We walk many blocks, Berger stumbles upon a curb, sneezes, an annoyingly tiny sneeze. I say, Bless you, he waves his hand.

"I do believe in God, yes."

"That's good, I suppose."

"Yes, I had an American girlfriend."

"And that's why you . . . "

"Well, I was . . . how you say, *beat up* with desire."

"Pussy-whipped."

Berger laughs, waves his hand, then sneezes again. Like a caught rat, it sounds. One eye watches me search my pants pockets; I find nothing.

"I have a handkerchief. 'Tis okay." He doesn't use it, wipes his nose with the back of his hand. "This American girlfriend, she was religious. A Christian Scientist."

"Don't they give everything they earn to the . . . "

"Yes, they give testimonies."

"How do you know Lidya?"

"Lidya, she is not part of this history."

"How far is your sister?"

"Not far, only here. But God, I do believe is a . . . collective soul. All of us, little bits of mind, lost, yes?"

"Lost?"

"Until we find our way of thought back to each other again. Ah, here it 'tis."

He gestures his odd way again, an arm, one eye at the entrance, the other rests on the flowers.

"The American girlfriend. She grew up in a loving house."

"All hunky-dory?"

"How do you say? Hunk-door . . . "

"Hunky-dory, peachy keen. Everything perfect."

"Ah yes, this she would seem. Come. This way, please."

He opens the door for me. The smell assaults us.

"My sister's friend, a composer, he makes perfume, yes. A special scent for each friend. Touching, isn't 'tit?"

Touching that he mentions the perfume but not the horrid stench it fails to hide. Berger, still extends his arm, I walk down the corridor which is mustard-colored, matte green potted plants line either side.

"I suppose they don't need light, these plants?"

"Oh no. My sister is a perfect mother . . . of plants. Even in illness." Berger lowers his voice. "She makes *ex*-quisite dolls as well, yes."

He raps on the door at the end of the hallway. A ghastly

murmur bids us to enter.

"I have brought a friend, Sunnie."

Sunnie is huge, with long hands to match. She overflows the bed. Her eyes are brilliant emerald, her smile thin, but warm.

"How do you do?" she nods. In German she asks Berger a question that makes him laugh. I want to leave immediately.

"She wants to know if I tell you she is contagious."

"Is she?"

"No, no. Of course not. She joked this way with my American girlfriend. She joked her about . . . what is it . . . 'thinking away the illness.' "

"Tell her I'd like to get out of here."

Berger says something to her, and they laugh.

"She wants to know if I tell you, yet, about Lidya."

"What about her?" I wish suddenly that I had brought my camera, as well as the eye. I would like to put it in the palm of his hand, tell him to hold it out in front of me in the ray of light that crosses Sunnie's bed just over her right hip and her left thigh. Tell her to smile again, the way she did when I took her huge hand in mine.

"They were friends long ago. That's how I met Lidya. I had both my eyes then. I was quite . . . handsome. But too quiet. Ah. Too quiet, too *young* for her."

"What is it you want, then? You want Lidya to come see her, is that it?" I look at the dresser, the pushed-in cloth faces of the many dolls, their hard legs of plastic.

"No, no. You know my father also knew Lidya quite well. *Too* well, in fact." One eye looks into mine with sudden hatred, the other stares lovingly at my hand.

Sunnie grabs my wrist, too strongly, pulls me to the bed.

"Tell her I hate it when people touch me."

Berger laughs, one eye now casually on me, the other on Sunnie's sheets. She tells him something quickly; urgently, her brows meet center.

"Actually, my friend, she wants you to touch her forehead. Gently please. Only lay your hand across it there, as if she has fever you might cool away."

The skin there is soft, I can feel the lines against my palm, as she breathes. She murmurs again in that frightening tongue I heard from behind the door. As I take my hand away she claps it back almost violently.

"Berger," she utters with desperation.

"She wants to remember you something. Only a minute, please my friend." He closes his eyes, turns toward the window. "Years ago on the boat of our father, there is an explosion. He was taking us from our mother, and he kept us there with all of our possessions. There is an explosion on the boat . . . that killed him. Sunnie makes herself ill, so many years, trying to remember, yes. What it 'tis he said."

The smell of the perfume is so thick in the room with the light caressing the dust. My palm sweats with the heat of her brain working like that. I try, with my palm, to take a picture of the mechanism beneath.

"She thinks you have it, yes? What my father said, how it rolls from his mouth as he lays there. Dying. I do not see him. Sunnie sees him. There is blood in my eyes. I do not remember. But she thinks you have it, my friend."

"I have your eye, Berger," I say suddenly. "It is home at Lidya's. I found it little more than a week ago. It was on her boat."

"You cannot have my eye, my friend. Here they are, they

look at you. My third eye, ah . . . 'tis long gone, it 'tis dead with our father, yes. It burns as many things on that boat burned. Many more things should have burned on that boat, as well. Like my father's letters to Lidya. Letters when she and Sunnie were no more than . . . what 'tis it? . . . 12?"

"I have to go."

And I rush out of the room, down the corridor, knocking over a pot, and out of the front door, bounding the steps. If I wanted to be that close to a father's legacy of guilt, I could have stayed at home with my mother.

Berger doesn't come after me. But I wait for him blocks and blocks away in my favorite courtyard near the Delacroix museum. A young Japanese man strokes a sweet flamenco guitar, pigeons gather; a woman sits on a bench that addresses the flowers at her feet. Perfect photograph. Like Lidya, as I first met her. I know this is why she keeps me so close to her heart. She said I found her there, in that polaroid, the first one I took before we began the shoot. She was at once that little girl and the old woman as she meets her end. And everything in between. She had all of her missing bits, she says were long ago *given,* not taken, away.

So what? I think, if Berger's father was in love with her? So what if he actually *took* her? People do survive that kind of thing.

I step toward the birds so I can hear the clutter of their wings as they take off in flight. As their wings meet the hollow of the instrument, there's a vibration in my stomach, I put my hand there, the tip of my fingers touching my breast pocket, and I realize the eye *is* there.

I turn around, and Berger stands there, feet apart. He smiles, then lifts his arms as if to embrace the air. Through the trees, from beyond Berger, the light hits me like the moment on that deck of the boat. Suddenly he disappears. And so my hand is back on Sunnie's forehead. I can see their father. Sure. But what does it matter what he said? Would it bring back all they had lost? Could it really give them *peace?*

I let the eye drop, and it rolls not so far from where I stand. And I'm not so far. I'm not so very far from where I stand.

About the Author

Lisa Teasley is a native of Los Angeles, California where she currently lives. Her fiction has appeared in numerous anthologies and publications such as *Step Into a World: A Global Anthology of the New Black Literature, Brown Sugar* and *Between C & D*. She has won the May Merrill Miller and the *Amaranth Review* awards for fiction. This is her first collection.